CONFLICT, PASSION, *and* PAIN

CONFLICT, PASSION, *and* PAIN

Thomas Edward Poe

ISBN: 978-1-63732-255-0   (Paperback Edition)
ISBN: 978-1-63732-258-1   (Hardcover Edition)
ISBN: 978-1-63732-254-3   (E-book Edition)

Some characters and events in this book are fictitious. Any similarity to real persons, living or dead, is coincidental and not intended by the author.

Book Ordering Information

Phone Number: 315 288-7939 ext. 1000 or 347-901-4920
Email: info@globalsummithouse.com
Global Summit House
www.globalsummithouse.com

Printed in the United States of America

CHAPTER

I

"Eli, this is Tony. Has anyone seen or heard from Dee?"

"No, I haven't heard a word from anybody," replied Eli.

"But it's been almost seven months, surely somebody must have heard something!" cried Tony. The frustration in Tony's voice mounted as he continued his relentless pursuit to find Dee.

There was a two-year age difference between Eli and Tony. They liked each other and shared many personal experiences, but since Dee's disappearance, Eli had been cold and distant.

"I know, Tony. I am very sorry."

As Tony cradled the phone, he was almost overcome by disappointment and panic that the news was the same as the days and weeks before from Jan, Eli's sister. He buried his head into the pillow wondering if he could live another minute without knowing where she was, why she left without a word, and if he would ever see her again.

In his desperation, he shouted aloud, "I thought we loved each other!"

Their last night together was no different from the many other loving and passionate evenings they'd had. There was no hint that anything was wrong. The last few weeks, he tried to think of all of the reasons why this was happening but always came up empty. At the time, he became angry at the thought that she knew Valentine's Day would be their last together. All of his frustration, anger, and disappointment always ended with "why?"

As he lay dreaming about the love he and Dee had shared for four years, he was unaware that Mrs. Grant had entered the room. He was startled by her presence.

"I am sorry, Tony," explained Mrs. Grant. "When you didn't answer my knocks, I was worried."

She gave Tony a puzzled look. "Child, I hope you feel better than you look. You look terrible. You have been in that bed for a week; you won't answer your calls; you don't want to see your friends, not even that pretty one that's been coming by. The doctor gave you a clean bill of health, so what's really wrong with you? It must be a girl."

Without answering, Tony turned his face to the wall hoping to find some of the sleep that had escaped him since Dee's sudden disappearance.

Entering his senior year in high school, Tony had been living on his own for more than two years. He wanted to prove something to his mother. His father was murdered when he was nine. He watched his mother struggle trying to work to raise a family of three. Because he was alone much of the time, Tony practically raised himself. Starting at twelve, during the summer, he worked at a service station and a grocery store during the winter months. He was an excellent worker. He was dedicated, dependable, and considered by all adults who knew him, "a good boy." He had a special thing for females; he truly loved them.

Before renting from the Grants, he had rented a room across town in a building that only rented to working women. The most pleasant moments he remembered from the room across town were the special times he spent with Dee. One of the rules was that he could not have female company. If he was caught violating this rule, he would be kicked out by the owner; therefore, he had to plan carefully. At other times, the noise and the lack of privacy were almost unbearable.

In the beginning, he enjoyed the competition among the women for his attention, but as time passed, it lost much of its glitter; especially after one of the women entered the hallway bathroom he was occupying and straddled him while he was sitting on the commode until her passion was filled. Tony was terribly confused by the event. Even though ambivalent, he was certain that it would not happen again, certain, also, that he would not tell.

Renting from the Grants was more like the family environment Tony always wanted but never had. They were nice people from the West Indies who came to this northern Illinois industrial town because of its job opportunities. Mr. Grant worked in a factory. As for Mrs. Grant, Tony never knew exactly what she did because she was always in and out and about. The room was $12.50 a week with dinner. The rules were fair; no females after midnight and not more than two visitors at one time.

Another week had passed, still no word about Dee. Soon, Tony would make the call he had been making almost every day for seven months which seemed more like an eternity.

Tony felt there was something different about this day, a new feeling, a hope—a need to move on, maybe even anger as thoughts of desertion and rejection began to take hold replacing the self-pity and despair of days past. Tony had been remembering the words of wisdom received from a "bum" who claimed to have earned a college degree, a Ph.D. to be exact.

He remembered his first encounter with his disheveled, unkempt friend at the local bus station. Tony was playing baseball on a pinball machine when this white male of about thirty-five leaned up against the machine causing it to tilt.

"Man, look what you've done! You've messed up my game!" Tony exclaimed. "So what?" he retorted. "You have won enough free games to play all night. I've been watching you hustle people on that machine. You'd better watch it. You are headed for trouble," warned the bum.

"It's none of your damn business," Tony replied with fire in his eyes.

"You're a smart one," stated the bum, not giving an inch.

Since that first encounter in a far corner of a sparsely populated bus station, they became friends of sorts. After observing each other for a few evenings, the bum made his move.

"Say, kid, I am sorry."

"It's okay," replied Tony in a rather cautious tone.

"Kid, why do you come here almost every evening? What do your parents say? What about your homework?"

Tony became slightly annoyed by the sudden barrage of questions. "Not that it's any of your business, but I come here to eat. My parents don't say anything because I live alone, and as for my homework, I am an honor student. Now, do you have any more questions?"

This man, who refused to give his name, was determined to take the sting out of Tony's voice and manner. As days passed, they were talking and sharing food, always at Tony's expense.

Indeed, there was plenty to remember about this mystery man who disappeared as quickly as he appeared.

His advice was: "Kid, remember that in any relationship, you must ask yourself two questions. First, is it good to you? And secondly, is it good for you? Should you answer either of these questions 'no', walk away from whomever or whatever and never look back."

Intellectually, the advice sounded good, but Tony was not sure how to act on it. He did wonder how this seemingly intelligent and smart man happened to be in his current situation. Tony was somewhat surprised and angered at his feelings of disappointment when the bum failed to show again.

He said to himself, "He didn't smell so bad after all."

Thus ended the saga of the boy and the bum.

As he reached for the phone, he noticed his hands shaking so violently that he replaced it. After three attempts, the phone rang, but only once before being interrupted by the operator, "What number please?"

Tony repeated the number in a trance-like state, his heart pounding as if it was going to jump from his chest.

The operator continued, "The number you dialed has been changed. At the owner's request, it is unlisted."

Tony's body went limp as if it had been delivered a blow rendering him unconscious. Had he not been able to slump into a nearby chair, the fall to the floor would not have been noticed as his body was numb from pain.

Tony was not immediately aware of time or place. It took a knock on the door to bring him back to reality.

"Tony, is your phone off the hook?" asked Mrs. Grant.

"Yes, I am sorry. I must have knocked it off." Almost immediately, his blood began to boil as thoughts raced through his head. He was being taken over by an over-powering kind of energy. He hurriedly slipped into a shirt, picked up his car keys, and bolted out of his room through the living room to his car.

Why had the phone number changed? Did this mean that Dee was back? He must find out! Tony drove like a man possessed. What was he going to say? What was he going to do? All of a sudden, he was panic-stricken. He pulled to the side of the road to ponder a most unbearable thought. Tony spoke aloud as if he was not alone, "What if Dee's family has moved?" He realized that his only hope or link to Dee was through her family, mainly Eli or Jan. "God," he cried. "What happens if I never see her again? No! No!" he shouted aloud, pounding the steering wheel.

Horns were blaring and voices were shouting. Looking up into the rearview mirror, he saw traffic backed up as far as he could see. He turned the ignition key to get started, not realizing the engine was already running. Without hesitation, the journey was continued; however, as he came closer to arriving at his destination, he was not so sure he really wanted to continue.

As the journey continued, he became quite apprehensive as to what he might or might not find. The fear of finding the truth was overridden by the need to know the truth. The closer he came to reaching his destination, the more he could feel the pounding of his heart in his hands while gripping the steering wheel.

"Oh my God! There it is. Let her be there! Let them be there!" Tony pulled into the driveway peering through the windshield to look for any sign of movement. He was relieved to find that there were curtains still on the windows. He opened the car door very slowly, hanging on tightly to maintain his balance as his knees were made of rubber. In his mind, he wanted to rush inside to find the truth, but his legs were not moving. After gaining his composure, he was ready for whatever awaited him. On the way to the front door, he counted every step, still not knowing what he would say or what he would do.

While he was approaching the door, it swung open. Eli must have been watching Tony through the window. Tony was greeted by Eli.

"Hello, Tony, this is a surprise. What are you doing here?"

"I tried to call, but the operator said that your number had changed," Tony explained.

"Come in," said Eli.

Tony and Eli went into the living room where they were joined by Eli's younger sister, Jan, and his brother, Ted. Their mother was working and didn't get home until later in the day. Tony knew that whatever was going on, the mother was in charge. Although they had a good relationship, he thought, he felt something had changed, and not knowing the nature of the change made Tony very nervous.

Eli was a little uneasy, especially when Jan and Ted entered the room. Jan was a little lady at thirteen. She always liked seeing and talking with Tony. Ted was a very busy eleven, but somewhat shy. He would always run from room to room, crawl on the floor, turn flips, or do something typical of his age. Eli was fifteen, sort of the man of the house. Sitting there in the room with them, Tony felt good, at ease, for he had truly missed them. Jan was sweet and loving as always, as he remembered. She had the most beautiful smile and a most unforgettable laugh.

"Don't see you anymore, Tony. What have you been doing?"

"Just working, that's all," he replied.

Normally, when Tony would visit, Ted was always in and out of the room, but this time, he sat and listened to all of the small talk as if he would miss something if he left the room. Tony wouldn't dare ask about Dee in Ted's presence.

Standing up, Tony said, "It was nice seeing you all again."

"I am walking Tony to the car. You all stay here; I'll be right outside," Eli asserted.

Once outside, Eli confirmed what Tony had suspected all along. "Tony, Mom don't want us to give you any information about Dee. She doesn't want you to call anymore. That's why the number was changed. She will be mad when she finds out that you were here today."

"Eli, do you know where Dee is? Is she okay?"

"Listen, Tony, I know where she is, but if I tell you, Mom will know it was me. Dee is okay, I can tell you that," Eli commented cautiously.

"What is she doing? Why did she leave?"

"Look man, I don't know," replied Eli hastily.

"Eli, please do me a big favor," Tony asked, giving Eli a piece of paper. "This is my number and address. Give it to her, and tell

7

her to please call or write. Man, I am going crazy. I have to know what's going on."

Eli took the paper saying, "I'll try, but I am not promising anything, okay?"

"Yeah, but you will try, won't you?" Tony and Eli waved goodbye as he drove away. He was feeling better, different.

As he drove away, he realized that he was still confused about Dee's sudden departure. There were no rumors or speculation among their friends. Although things were not clear, he was glad that Mrs. Davis was not at home during his visit. Delores, the older sister, was in college. Mrs. Davis was a very hard-working woman. Tony admired her for working so hard to keep the family together; however, there were times when she arrived home from work in a very serious mood, and everybody stayed out of her way. Jan had her mother's smile and looks, only Mrs. Davis did not use her smile very much. Tony had known the family about five years. During this time, he had never seen or heard much about the father who still lived somewhere in the South. After the murder of his father, followed by an unpleasant stepfather experience, Tony never thought much about fathers. Anyway, the few memories he had of his father were not very nice.

When Tony returned to his room, he found Margo waiting. She was talking with Mrs. Grant who appeared to be in a hurry to leave.

"You left in such a hurry, I didn't expect you back so soon. Is everything alright?" Mrs. Grant had such a pleasant disposition. She made everyone feel special and welcomed. In her sweet West Indian accent, she could also be quite nosey. Mrs. Grant liked Margo, and she always found some place to go when Margo came to visit. "Call your job. They are looking for you," yelled Mrs. Grant on her way out.

Margo was two years older than Tony and much more experienced in the ways of the world and relationships. There were rumors that Margo had a hot romance going with an older man named Melvin. Tony had seen him around many times. As a matter of fact, Tony, at one time, had a crush on his sister. Anyway, Tony's thoughts were so completely dominated by Dee that he only gave the rumors a passing thought. Margo was gorgeous from any direction; she knew it, and at times, flaunted it. She lived just across the street from where Tony worked. In the evenings, when he was almost always alone, she was his constant companion. She was visiting her sister and brother-in-law for the summer.

The service station was a hang out for guys of all ages most evenings and Saturdays. You could hear all of the latest gossip, settle arguments, and get plenty of free unsolicited advice any time. During the busiest times, Margo would dress up and walk past the station on her way to the grocery store two doors down. She knew how to dress; every strand of her short brown hair was in place, and when she walked, everybody looked. Her body was perfectly proportioned, and the clothes she wore, even though always appropriate and in good taste, put her on display. Tony remembered the impact she had on Rob, one of the station owners, one Saturday afternoon.

As she walked by, Rob commented, "God has done that girl a real injustice by making her so beautiful." Rob was well known as a ladies' man by everyone except his wife.

"Well, hello, stranger. You've been avoiding and neglecting me. Do you want to tell me why? Is your schoolmate back in town?"

He could tell Margo was in one of her "catty" moods. She wanted attention or a fight, or maybe both, but he was unsure which. It was difficult to deny her what she wanted.

"From what I hear, you haven't been neglected," Tony retorted sarcastically.

Margo, moving closer, put her arms around Tony's neck while touching him with the lower part of her body. She whispered, "Tony, I don't want to fight with you."

As she kissed him, he knew that fighting was the last thing he wanted to do. In a flash, they were passionately ignited. The passion and desire seemed more intense than any previous time. Since their meeting, five months ago, they had never spent more than two days apart. They spent the rest of the afternoon in bed making up for lost time.

"Will I see you tomorrow?" she asked.

"You can see me as much and as often as you like. I love being with you, and how you make me feel," Tony responded.

But somehow Margo needed more assurance. "More than you love Dee? Maybe you are just waiting for her to return so that you can get back with her." Margo was becoming more annoyed as she spoke.

"I don't want to talk about her, Margo. What's wrong with you anyway? She's not here, and I don't know where she is. For all I know, she's gone to stay. Let's talk about you and me, not Dee!"

"Tony, I want you to clearly understand that I will not be used by you or anyone else. I want you to promise me that you will never see her again. I want you to promise NOW!" shouted Margo.

"Okay, okay, I promise," he agreed.

Margo appeared to be happy with his promise. Tony had never seen that side of her, and he was willing to do or say whatever it took to calm her down. She seemed to be on the verge of becoming physical before he made the promise. The fire he saw in her eyes was frightening. Margo dressed and left quietly. Her behavior worried Tony.

If Dee was to appear tomorrow, he knew that he would not be able to keep his promise. If he couldn't have Dee, he wasn't about to let Margo get away. Exhausted and completely fulfilled, Tony drifted off to a deep sleep. The next few days were great for Tony. Margo admitted to dating Melvin because she thought Tony didn't want her, but she promised to never date him or anyone else again.

CHAPTER

II

Days were passing in rapid succession, but still there was no word from Dee. Although he and Margo were spending most of their time together, thoughts of Dee would grip him without mercy at times. With each passing day, he began to think more and more about football, school, and college. Tony was one of the more popular boys in school, very well liked by both girls and boys. He was considered to be very good looking, friendly, and a gentleman. He was looking forward to his last year, and seeing many of his classmates to hear all of the "tall tales of summer."

Twice-a-day football practices were over with less than two weeks before the start of school. During this time and until the beginning of classes, Tony's work schedule had been changed from three in the afternoon until nine at night with the usual eight hours on Saturdays and Sundays.

On this particular day, Tony arrived at work early. He was surprised to see so many people hanging around so early, especially the older crowd. Usually, the group didn't gather until five or six. They appeared to be waiting for Tony. The Harris and the Silas brothers were there with sly grins on their faces.

"Hey, Tony, Margo wants to see you," John Silas offered in a voice that everyone could hear; simultaneously, everyone burst into laughter.

Tony was puzzled and annoyed. He was met at the door by Rob, who rushed him inside closing the door to avoid interruption.

"Rob, what's going on? Why is everyone acting so crazy?"

"Is that Melvin's car across the street at Margo's house?" Rob asked while looking across the street.

"Yes, I think so," Tony replied, still not sure what was happening.

"Well, it is, and everybody is waiting to see how you are going to handle it," Rob commented calmly.

"Why should I do anything, Rob?"

"You might have to do something. Melvin is coming, and he's been over there waiting a long time."

Melvin knocked on the door, enjoying all of the attention. His attitude urged them on. He was about three inches taller and thirty pounds heavier than Tony, but like many others of any size, Tony was a fighter with a killer instinct. Rob looked a little concerned as Tony moved to open the door. Melvin appeared, looking quite confident, maybe he felt being three years older and bigger automatically gave him an advantage.

"Margo wants to see you across the street," Melvin said, speaking as if he was delivering a message to a child.

"Tell her I'll be there in a minute," Tony replied through a half-opened door.

Once outside, he heard voices from the group saying that Melvin had a gun, some said a knife. After hearing these comments, Tony decided not to take any chances. He returned to the tool rack and slid an eighteen-inch tire iron up his sleeve. He was not afraid to fight, and everyone knew it. Although most in the group were bigger and older, no one was anxious to fight Tony, several had tried and lost.

The walk across the street was long and his heart was pounding so hard and so loud that he could almost feel his entire body shake. It was easily the longest walk of his life. Tony could feel the eyes of the crowd on his back as he moved slowly across the street to the front door. He was almost paralyzed with apprehension and anticipation. He would have preferred to be anyplace else, but here he was, not quite sure what he was doing or why he was doing it, but with the world watching, he had no choice. He had to find the courage. Fighting over a woman was something Tony did not believe in, but he remembered the advice of his brother, "If you have to fight, get the first blow, and fight to win."

Rather than knock, Tony opened the door and entered unnoticed. No one was in the living room, but he heard voices coming from Margo's bedroom. The voices sounded angry.

Again, Tony entered without knocking. "Say man, don't you know how to knock?"

Ignoring Melvin, he said, "Margo, you sent for me, here I am." Tony spoke, noticing a slight tremble in his voice.

She looked a mess and the room was also a mess. They had made love either before or after the argument.

Melvin was not to be ignored. "I hear you have been seeing my woman, Tony."

"If you are talking about Margo, I never knew she was your woman."

"Okay, let's settle this right now," stated Melvin. "Margo, tell him right now that you love me, and that you don't want to see him again," Melvin demanded.

"Melvin, I can't do that, I am not sure. I am all confused!" she shouted as she hurried out of the room in tears.

"As far as I am concerned, Melvin, you can have her. From the looks of her and this room, you've already had her. Good luck to both of you," Tony said as he was leaving the room.

"She would have chosen me anyway. Just make sure you don't try to see her again or..."

"Or what, Melvin? You are not going to do anything! You wanted her, now you've got her. She's all yours, but don't ever make the mistake of threatening me!" shouted Tony holding back the urge to strike Melvin.

On his way to the front door, Melvin cried out, "She said that I was the best lover she ever had."

"So what?! She said the same thing to me!" Tony shouted slamming the door on his way out.

For the next few days, Margo and Melvin were almost inseparable. Sometimes, they would come to buy sodas or gas. Melvin would always make sure Tony was there alone to serve him. Margo was always sitting up close to him. She never appeared to be enjoying it as much as Melvin. She had tried to talk with Tony several times since the confrontation, but he would not receive her visits or calls. Tony knew that he could have her back for the asking, but she had lied and cheated, and he was not about to forgive her. Anyway, he was somewhat relieved, although his pride was hurt. Now, if Dee returned, he would be free of Margo.

Tony anxiously awaited the beginning of school. The first day was a week away. He wondered why Dee hadn't called, because Eli had given her the message. This had been a very difficult summer for him. Not too many things had gone well, and he was glad to see it come to a close. It was a hurting summer.

CHAPTER

III

The most talked about issues among Tony's circle of friends were the nice weather and questions about whether or not Dee would be returning to school. They had not seen Tony and Dee together and, for the last month or more, had started asking questions. Dee's name always surfaced when Tony was with friends. Some saw his pain, while others made light of the matter.

The weather was a popular subject with both the young and old. This was perfect autumn weather; the ground was covered with golden-brown leaves, with bright sunshine, clear blue skies, and mild temperatures. It had been hard for Tony to go to work lately. *Hell, it's too nice to work*, he thought. These thoughts were going through his mind as he listened to the Cubs and Dodgers. Margo had called a couple of times, but as usual, he wouldn't talk to her. The phone rang, but again, he wouldn't answer it because he didn't want to talk to Margo.

He looked at the clock and thought that the time was racing in order to rush him off to work. *About forty-five minutes before going to work,* he thought. The phone began to ring again. He took his time answering it because he suspected Margo.

"Hello," he answered in a matter-of-fact tone.

"May I speak with Tony?"

"Oh my God! Dee?"

"Yes, Eli gave me your message," she offered.

"Dee, oh my God, this is really you?" Tony cried, unable to hold back the tears.

"Please, Tony. Look, I'm sorry for leaving without a word. I know you've gone through hell, but so have I. When I left, I was almost three months pregnant. I wanted to tell you, but Delores and Mom said that I shouldn't. That's why I went away to have your baby. Please don't cry; I know you are mad it me," Dee explained. It was if she needed to explain her absence in one breath.

Tony was still rocked by her call, clutching the phone, but unable to speak.

Dee continued. "Tony, I signed papers to give our baby away, but I can change my mind, I think. Please say something."

"Honey, why didn't you tell me? We could have gotten married. I love you. Dee, I missed you so much; I have been going crazy! Where are you?"

"I can't tell you where I am, Tony, I promised."

"Are you coming home?" he asked.

"Tony, I can't tell you anything. Delores and Mom would die if they knew I was talking to you."

"Dee, please give me a number where I can call or an address, I will write to you,' he begged.

"No, I can't give you a number or an address. Tony, what shall I name the baby? What about the baby, Tony? Do you want me to see if we can get the baby back?" her questions were in rapid succession without giving him an opportunity to answer.

"Yes, we will get married and get our baby. Dee, will you name the baby after me?"

"Yes, okay, Tony, I will name him after you. He looks just like you."

"Oh, Dee, I am so glad you called. When will I hear from you again? I don't want to lose you again,' he pleaded.

"I love you, Tony. No matter what happens, remember, I love you. I've got to go now," she whispered softly.

Tony held on to the phone a while, happy he had heard from Dee, but he felt somewhat depressed and helpless. With no way to contact her, it was like he was being deserted a second time.

"A baby," he said aloud to himself.

Tony went through the next few days in a fog. He had missed a couple of practices, and the coach warned that the next would be his last. Margo and Melvin split, and she found all kinds of reasons to drop by the station hoping to get his attention. Sometimes, Tony would come to work and find her in the office talking with Rob and Clettis, his brother-in-law. Nothing worked as Tony completely ignored her. She asked Tony to forgive her, and he did. But Margo wanted more than forgiveness, she wanted him back.

"Listen, Margo," he explained on the phone, "you may not believe me, but I do forgive you. It's just that I don't feel the same about you anymore. We can't get back together." His answer appeared to agitate her.

"Are you saying it's over?"

"Yes, Margo, it's over," he confirmed.

Tony was glad their conversation was on the phone as she became very angry and abusive.

"Listen, you bastard, it's not over until I say it's over," she responded angrily.

"Margo, it's over," he calmly replied.

"If it's the last thing I do, I will make you pay," she promised slamming the phone in his ear.

The first day of school was great! All of his teachers seemed nice. Tony had really been looking forward to renewing old acquaintances. The first football game was only two days away. Tony was a good athlete. He lettered in three sports. He saw football as his way towards success. Playing both offense and defense gave him plenty of exposure. His dream was to use his scholarship to become a journalist. Overall, Tony felt good and comfortable in all aspects of being in school. He felt that it was the most productive and constructive part of his life. It was as if school put his life in some kind of order.

Tony arose early to prepare for the second day of school. He wanted to stop by his sister's house before picking up his companions: Peter, Scott, Rosey, and Maxie. Although they were considered friends, Tony mostly saw them when they would cram into his customized black Mercury every morning heading to school. It was always a very lively trip with plenty of joyful badgering, gossip, and speculations about any and everything, usually led by Peter.

Marie was Tony's oldest sister. She was always easy to talk to without unwanted advice and judgment. He always enjoyed spending time with her. Her cooking was the best. On this particular morning, he knew that Clettis, his brother-in-law, would have left for work, and that he would have Marie by himself. He also knew that breakfast was ready. She must have seen his car through the window because as he entered the yard, she opened the door to greet him.

"Come in, stranger, long time no see. How've you been? Want some breakfast?" She was always glad to see Tony.

"Yeah, I'd like some breakfast," he replied as they hugged each other.

"Are you glad to be back in school?" she asked.

"Yes, I like school, but it's not the same without Dee. Sis, she called me a few days ago, but she wouldn't tell me where she was. She said she left because she was pregnant and that she has already had the baby, a boy. She also said that she had given him up for adoption. If we get married, we may be able to get our baby back. What do you think?" he asked, looking up from the table at his sister for an answer.

Marie, in the meantime, was trying very hard to retain her composure after being bombarded with this shocking information. "My God, Tony, you just walk in and drop all of this on me and want to know what I think. Wow! I don't know," she said, as she looked for someplace to sit. She was visibly shaken. "Tony, I really don't know what you should do, but do you think marriage is the answer? What about school, and your scholarship? Have you told Mom yet? What about Dee's mom? You and Dee really need to talk about this situation. You two are faced with a very big decision."

"I'd like to sit down and talk to her, but I don't know where she is or how to reach her. I don't even know if she will be coming back home. Sis, I really don't know what to do."

"Well, little brother, as it stands, you can't do anything except continue on in school and pray."

"Sis, tell me something. If you were going to have a baby by someone you loved, would you let him know?"

"Honey, I know how you feel about Dee, and I think I know how she feels about you, but given her situation with the same circumstances, I have absolutely no idea what I would do. I will tell you one thing: don't judge her until you know all of the facts."

After talking with Marie, he always felt more at ease and positive about life; however, he was keenly aware that she wasn't too excited about him quitting school or the idea of marriage.

Peter was usually the last to be picked up every morning. He was the "joker" among the group. There was nothing he couldn't turn into a joke. No one wanted to be the subject of his jokes because he didn't know when to stop. Peter knew everybody, and he could con and scheme with the very best. Scott was just the opposite. He was the quiet one of the group. Scott was also the "brains" of the group, and the object of many of Peter's jokes. Tony and Scott were more alike and more serious than the rest of the group. Since Scott was the first to have a TV, Tony and Peter spent more time at his house watching television, mostly wrestling. Scott had two younger brothers. His father had passed away leaving his mother to raise three sons.

Rosey had several brothers and sisters. Tony liked his older sister at one time, but somehow they drifted apart. The attraction was weak. Rosey was a little on the quiet side unless aroused by Peter. Finally, there was Maxie, "the fox". Tony knew very little about her accept that she seemed more mature, and that she always appeared to be, or wanted to be, in control. Tony liked her, but he was afraid to let her know. He felt that she would either laugh at him or tell the group who would certainly laugh at him. Maxie always talked about older boys with cars and money. Her apparent experience threatened Tony.

After everyone was in the car, Tony noticed that everyone was much quieter than usual, especially Peter. There was a little small talk about school, teachers, courses, and of course, the opposite sex. Traffic was moving at a steady pace. On this particular morning, all seemed well with Tony.

As he approached the stop where Eli and Jan caught the bus, he prepared to wave as he always did. He had his arm out of the window to wave, but when he looked in their direction, he was shocked to see Dee.

In his state of numbness, he must have looked away from the road too long because Peter grabbed the steering wheel shouting, "Fool, look where you're going!"

Tony recovered and pulled to the side of the road, trying to gather himself, and his reaction was enough to ignite the whole group.

Peter continued, "Say man, we know you're glad to see your old lady, but you don't have to get us all killed."

"So Dee is back in town," Rosey said, looking a little puzzled.

Looking at Tony, and how he was shaken, everyone started laughing as if they would burst; this was Peter's moment.

"Did you see how Tony Paul looked when he saw Dee?" Peter asked, using Tony's entire name for impact. "I thought he had seen a ghost." The laughter was almost deafening as Peter made faces and gestures to describe Tony.

"Shut up! Shut up! Shut up!" Tony shouted angrily.

"Oh shit, he is mad now. We'd better keep quiet or Mr. Paul will have us walking to school," Peter commented almost jokingly.

Everyone continued having difficulty controlling the urge to laugh, but they all knew Tony was quite capable of throwing them out.

"Tony, want me to drive?" asked Maxie.

"No thanks, I'll drive," he replied.

"Well, what are we waiting for?" asked Scott almost apologetically.

"We are waiting until I am ready. Anybody don't like it can catch the bus," retorted Tony.

"I told you all to keep quiet," teased Peter.

Tony couldn't continue on as if he hadn't seen Dee. He drove to the next corner, turned to circle the block.

"Everybody get out. Catch the bus. I'll pick you all up in the morning," he stated while reaching across to open the passenger door.

They all hurriedly started to get out.

"Say, Tony, my man, we were just kidding. Can't you take a joke? Where is your sense of humor?" quizzed Peter while getting in a few last-second "digs" making sure he was well out of Tony's reach.

Tony circled the block and stopped across the street where Dee, Eli, and Jan were standing. As he approached Dee, he could hear his heart pounding louder with each step that brought him closer to her. God! *She is more beautiful than I remembered*, he thought. She wore a green dress that exposed the upper portion of her well-developed chest. Her hair was up, a style he had never seen her wear, but he liked it although it made her look more than her age. Her lips, painted red, were full and luscious. He knew that she had seen him drive up across the street, but she never made a move to recognize his presence. She never looked in his direction.

Jan and Eli spoke, and he detected a friendliness that made him feel welcome.

When Dee spoke, her voice was barely audible. "Hi Tony," she whispered.

"Hello, this is a real big surprise. I am very happy to see you. Could I give you a ride to school?"

"No, Tony, I am going to catch the bus."

"Dee, can I talk to you? I need to talk to you."

"I am sorry, Tony, my bus is here."

As she walked away, he touched her hand gently. "Dee, why can't you ride with me? Please go with me," he pleaded.

"I have to go," she said, at the same time turning to step on the bus.

Tony hadn't heard a word from Dee since they talked about the baby. He wondered and worried about what was going on. The walk back across the street to his car was very long and lonely. He didn't have any idea that he would see her or that she would be so cold. She almost acted as if she hated him. Her behavior was baffling, to say the least. Disappointed and frustrated, he decided to take his sister's advice, not to judge.

Tony pulled out into the traffic to continue and saw Peter standing almost in the traffic lane directing him to the curb. When Tony stopped, everyone returned to their places.

"We saw what happened so we decided to wait," offered Maxie.

"Boy, Dee is back in town. That really was her, wasn't it?" asked a puzzled Scott, not sure of what he had seen.

"Man, I am sorry. I didn't know the situation was that serious," stated Peter, attempting to apologize for his previous behavior.

"That goes for me, too," interjected Rosey.

The remainder of the trip was in dead silence. Tony knew that what happened would be all over school in a couple of days, but he was much more worried about how to have a private talk with Dee. The next day, Dee refused to ride with him again. She also continued to refuse to come to the phone when he called. All he thought about was her.

The first football game produced an easy win, but the coach was not impressed with anyone's performance, especially Tony's. He also found it very difficult to concentrate on his studies. A couple of weeks went by with no change in his situation with Dee. He changed his work schedule hoping that he would be able to see her. He thought about how strange life had become. He wanted to be with Dee, and Margo wanted to be with him. Margo had been as persistent in her efforts to be with him as he was with Dee. He wasn't sure what he had done to deserve such treatment from Dee, but both he and Margo knew what had happened between them. Anyway, he never returned Margo's calls, but she was sure to show on the weekend at his work.

Since school was the only place he could possibly see Dee, weekends seemed to last forever. Tony realized that he had to move back near the west side of town because the convenience of being near work did not outweigh the fact that he was too close to Margo and too far from Dee. He would call the doctor to see if he could have his old room back. The doctor was surprised to hear from him and offered the room at the previous price. Tony accepted and moved the next day. It would be a relief to be away from the watchful eyes of Margo.

CHAPTER

IV

As Tony awakened Monday morning to prepare for school, he wondered what was ahead of him. He dashed out the door to pick up his friends in an unusually good mood. Passing Dee's bus stop on the way, he never looked her way, and everyone noticed.

Peter was very animated in showing his amazement. "Did you all see what I just saw?"

"Yes we did," the group replied almost in unison.

"Now you've got the right approach. Women can't stand to be ignored. Listen to me and we'll have her eating out of your hands," advised Peter.

"Peter," commented Maxie, reaching across the front seat to make Peter face her. "You only know one thing about women, and you probably ain't no good at that. Anyway, how do you know so much about women? As a matter of fact, from what I hear, you don't know anything."

Maxie had Peter on the run. Rosey and Scott were really enjoying the activity.

"Go on, Maxie, what's the word on Peter?" urged Rosey.

"Yeah, tell us everything," requested Scott.

"Maxie, you don't want to start me talking do you," threatened Peter.

"You don't know anything about me, Peter, so I am not worried."

The group joked and badgered each other during the entire trip, which made the time pass very quickly.

Tony had no idea why he passed Dee's stop all week without acknowledging her, or why he avoided her in the hallways at school. It was not part of a plan, but after doing it a few days, he couldn't think of a good reason to stop. Her sudden disappearance, sudden return, and her distant attitude had taken its toll, and Tony was beginning to change. He had hoped that after talking with her on the phone before she returned, they would talk about marriage and getting their child. He was willing to forgo the scholarship and college, although the thought of it all was quite frightening.

As days passed without resolution, he wondered if it would be wise to forget about Dee and the baby. He felt betrayed by Dee. After all, this wasn't the first time she had hurt him. He still remembered her affair with the sailor and one with a "lowlife" that lived near where he worked, plus a few questionable calls. Tony had been completely true to Dee up until she suddenly left town, but she couldn't come close to saying the same. Remembering the past, the bewilderment Tony once felt was slowly being replaced by anger and resentment. *To hell with her*, he thought, *I'm tired of hurting*.

School was just the medicine he needed to keep his mind occupied. He thought of Dee quite a lot, but he never made any attempt to call or to see her. Work, school, and football were most of his daily routine. The few times he saw her in passing were still very painful. Three weeks had passed since he first saw her at the bus stop. She seldom came up as a conversation piece on the way to school.

For some reason, Tony felt that any place would be better than being at school as he strolled towards second hour study hall. He remembered how he valued study hall because it allowed him to get all of his work done at school and without interruption. He rarely had to do homework away from school although he was an honor student. He had only one class where he had to put forth a 100% effort: botany. His teacher always tried to embarrass him in front of the class, especially with the girls as several of them were very friendly towards Tony. He would always ask questions of Tony, but he was never able to embarrass or catch Tony off guard.

As usual, he acknowledged several classmates and friends on his way to study hall. Without warning, he felt a gentle tap on his shoulder, and before turning around or hearing a voice, he instinctively knew it was Dee.

"I'd swear you were trying to avoid me. Are you?" she asked.

"Isn't that what you wanted? Remember, I did try to talk to you, but you acted like you didn't want to be bothered. What did you expect me to do?"

"I am very sorry, Tony. Things are such a mess."

"Dee, can we talk soon?"

"Yes, I will wait for you tomorrow after school in your car."

"Okay, I will see you after practice."

Tony was so excited that he could hardly control himself. It was the happiest day he had known for many months. Finally, he and Dee would get a chance to talk. By practice the next afternoon, the word had already spread that they were back together. Although they hadn't talked about it, Tony was sure that they would be as close as ever. As usual, he shared most of his news with his sister, Marie.

He rang the doorbell and waited.

"Well, good morning, come on in," she said, as she cheerfully welcomed him. "Would you like some breakfast?"

"No, Sis, not this morning."

"Are you sick or something? You don't want to eat," she quizzed with a puzzled look.

"Sis, I am going to talk with Dee today after school."

"Don't you see each other every day at school?"

"Well, yes we do, Sis, but we have never talked since she returned. Today, we are going to talk."

"Honey, I should have guessed it was something big to take away your appetite. What are you going to talk about?" she asked.

"Us, the baby, and marriage, I suppose. I don't know for sure. We will probably talk about everything."

"Tony, you and Dee are really good kids, but don't you think things are getting a little out of control, or maybe already out of control. You two are only children. A family is a big responsibility. How will you support them? You will need a place to stay, food, clothes, doctor bills, and many other things. How will you manage? Quitting school is not the answer. What about your future, college, scholarship, and plans?"

"Marie, I know all of those things; it's just something I have to do. Anyway, nothing is for sure right now," Tony commented while raising his hands as if to fend off Marie's questions.

"Come by tomorrow morning for breakfast. I will cook your favorite, okay?"

"Yeah, Sis, I'll see you then." Tony knew that the invitation for breakfast was partly out of kindness and also to get the results of the talk between him and Dee.

"Tony, you seem to be in a good mood this morning," remarked Rosey.

"I feel okay," Tony replied sensing something in Rosey's manner.

"Want to tell us why you're so happy, mister?" asked Scott.

Now, Tony was sure everyone knew he and Dee were talking.

"If you won't, I will," laughed Peter. "Hear this! Hear this! Mr. Tony and Miss Dee are back together again as of yesterday!"

"Peter, how do you know so much?"

"That's the word I got also," confirmed Maxie.

"He ain't denying it so it must be true," shouted Rosey.

The ride to school was very lively. Tony had told everyone that he would be picking them up five minutes earlier, but he refused to say why. He figured they would guess.

Dee and Tony passed each other a couple of times that day, but never said a word. He noticed that she looked at him the way she had so many times before, a look that always melted his heart. Class work was a total blank because all he could think about was being with Dee after school. He had been warned by Mr. Harris to concentrate on his studies and college. Mr. Harris also warned him that girls were a serious distraction and that being in love took too much time, thought, and energy. Everyone respected the old man's advice, but he had waited much too late for his wisdom to change what was happening in Tony's life.

Peter usually rode with Tony after practice, but on this day, Tony asked Peter to tell the coach he had to rush home.

"Man, are you crazy? The coach is going to be mad as hell. You are already on his list. You know you should go to practice. See your woman after practice," chided Peter.

After the last period, he rushed to catch Dee. He saw her walking down the stairs as he came near. Out of all the girls he had known, no one compared to Dee. There was something about her that was impossible for him to explain, maybe magic. All he knew was that he could never see enough of her. Even after five years, her presence still made his heart pound, his palms sweat, and gave him a general feeling of excitement and sweet anticipation that left him drained. She was always as ready for him as he was for her. Their lovemaking was always tender, passionate, and fulfilling. The gates of heaven would open with each embrace. Their passion and desire were of unreachable heights and depths.

Tony had missed her so much. As she came closer, he felt the pounding of his heart. He wanted to say something but feared that it would not be audible.

After clearing his throat, he commented almost in a whisper, "I am not going to practice so we can talk now if you'd like."

She was in a very cheerful and playful mood. Slipping her hand into his, she cooed, "Come walk me to my locker."

They walked hand in hand, applying varying degrees of pressure as they gazed into each other's eyes.

"You had better stop looking at me that way," she teased.

"Oh honey, I have missed you so much," Tony whispered, looking around to see if anyone could hear.

"I missed you too, Tony."

"Tell me something. Why have you been so cold towards me?" he asked.

"Let's go, I will explain everything."

"Okay if we go someplace where we can be completely alone?" Tony asked, not knowing what the answer would be.

"Yes, I'd like that very much, Tony."

Tony had been waiting for this day for quite some time; he and Dee would finally talk. He knew exactly where he would take her. It was their special place, a place where they had been many times. During the fall, it was almost always vacant. The park was beautiful. Brown leaves covered the ground. There were several small streams of water that would be frozen soon. It was the perfect place to talk. As he drove, they touched and kissed at almost every traffic stop. He touched her. She touched him, and they both went crazy with passion and desire.

Upon arriving at the park, they decided to talk in the car.

"Tony, I know that I've hurt you very much, and I am not proud of the way I have been acting since my return, but I promised Mother and Delores that I wouldn't see you again; otherwise, I would have been sent to live with family in Arkansas. We may have never seen each other again. I had to promise, Tony, I had to," she cried. Trembling through her tears, she continued, "I don't want you to be mad at me. Do you understand?"

Tony found it difficult to maintain his composure. "Yes, honey, I do understand. Please don't cry. Everything will be fine." Tony was holding her close, comforting her as she cried uncontrollably. It was if she had been holding back her emotions for just this moment.

They continued to embrace as he kissed her lips and her tears. "I saw you every day, and I wanted to talk to you, to explain. I never stopped loving you a minute. I could never stop loving you no matter what. It reached a point where I just couldn't take it anymore so here we are. The promises I made are impossible for me to keep. You mean everything to me. What are we going to do, Tony?"

"Why didn't you tell me you were pregnant?"

"I was afraid you wouldn't want me anymore. Anyway, I tried to tell you, but I just got scared. Things happened so fast that I didn't have time to think, so Mother and Delores arranged for me to go to this place where I could have the baby and still go to school. They said that if I had any contact with you, I would be sent to live with family. Tony, I was scared to death."

"It's over now, honey, we are together again and that's all that matters," he cradled her in his arms and rocked her as if she was a child.

"Dee, I am going to quit school and find a job so we can get married."

"We will both quit school, find jobs, and get our baby back," Dee firmly stated. "Tony, let's go for a walk."

He took the blanket from the trunk where it had been since they last shared it. They walked through the park until they were concealed. They lay on the blanket to fight the chill, but in an instant, they begin to embrace and express all of the love and emotion they had missed. Their passion exploded in supreme ecstasy. They expressed love, shared love, and gave love until all sense of time was lost.

"Tony, I love you very much. No words can express how I feel when we are together."

"I love you, too, honey. Let's never be apart again."

"Mother will know that we've been together, and she will be very upset. Are you going inside with me?"

"You bet; we will face her together, and let her know about our plans. I sort of told Marie," he confessed, looking for Dee's approval.

"Oh, how is Marie? What did she say? Tony, I am getting cold. Hold me a little while before we go. I am so happy we are together."

He held her very close for quite a while in complete silence. As they held on to each other, the beating of their hearts was the only sound heard above their feelings.

CHAPTER

V

It had been several months since Tony had seen Delores and Mrs. Davis. On this particular occasion, he certainly wasn't looking forward to seeing either. He had known the family a long time, and he was surprised and disappointed with the way the pregnancy was handled. Mrs. Davis was a hard-working, tough-minded person. On the way to Dee's house, he was wondering how this news would affect the family, especially Mrs. Davis. Talking about getting married was easy, but the thought of confronting Mrs. Davis provoked serious anxiety. The closer they came to the house, the more anxious Tony became. His mouth was dry, his voice wasn't right, and he was shaking all over. Dee must have noticed his nervousness.

"Are you afraid, Tony?"

"I am scared to death," he confessed. "You know your mother, how do you think she will act?"

"For sure, she will be upset," Dee assured. "But beyond that, I don't know."

"Some help you are," he said, his voice in high pitch.

Dee was laughing. "Tony, I can't believe it, you are really scared. I never knew you were afraid of Mother."

"That's because I never asked for your hand in marriage before."

They both laughed. "Dee, this Friday will be my last day of school. I will turn in my football gear tomorrow."

Dee was quite alarmed, "Are you sure you really want to do this? What about college. You have a great scholarship; you can't give up everything for me and the baby. You would never be happy. I won't let you."

"Honey, I am sure, and we have already had this discussion."

The walk to the door seemed to take forever. Tony had no idea what to expect, but he knew that he would soon find out. Mrs. Davis was waiting in the living room, very angry.

"I wondered how long it would take before you two got back together. Dee, what happened to your promise?"

"Mother, I really tried." Crying, she continued, "I don't want to hurt you, but I love Tony, and he loves me."

Mrs. Davis was standing, hands on hips, and displaying every ounce of her disappointment as Dee and Tony stood hand in hand.

"Where was he when you needed him? What was he doing while you were having his baby? Now, after all of the pain and suffering you two have caused this family, you act as if nothing happened. Where were you anyway, trying to have another baby?!" exclaimed a tearful Mrs. Davis.

"Mother, how could he do anything, he didn't even know I was pregnant," cried Dee.

"Mrs. Davis, Dee and I would like to get married and get our baby back."

After his words, Mrs. Davis gave them a long, serious stare. "What do you kids know about marriage and a family? Where will you live, better yet, how will you live? Tony, can you support a wife and a child?"

"Yes, ma'am, I can find a good job. We'll be okay," he said, speaking in a nervous and uncertain tone. It occurred to Tony that Marie had asked him the exact same questions.

"God help us all. Do you realize the kind of responsibility you are taking on?"

"Yes, ma'am, that's why I am quitting school," he offered.

"Mother, I will be quitting, also."

"Wait a minute, just you two wait a minute! What do you mean both of you are quitting school?"

"Yes ma'am," Tony replied.

"Child, does your mother know what you are planning to do?"

"No, ma'am, but my sister Marie knows."

"Let's get one thing straight right now," Mrs. Davis stated more calmly than before. "I am completely against you two seeing each other, and you both know why, but I have a feeling that you two will see each other no matter what I or anyone thinks, so here is what we are going to do. We will all get together this weekend after we have had some time to think things over. In the meantime, neither one of you will quit school until we all talk."

"Mrs. Davis," he responded, "I love Dee, and I will not change my mind. I want to marry her."

"Okay, Tony, I understand, but sometimes you kids think that there is only one way to solve a problem when there may be many. Let's get together Saturday afternoon." Mrs. Davis left the room immediately, leaving the door open. In a short while, Jan and Ted came into the room and sat quietly.

Dee and Tony didn't know what to think. They were surprised by Mrs. Davis's attitude towards the end of the conversation. She didn't appear to be as angry. Tony noticed a different kind of concern, one that he did not understand. They had not expected the talk to end in such a calm manner.

"What do you think, Tony?"

"I really don't know, but nothing can change my mind, and I will never give you up, never."

Dee walked Tony to his car. They walked very slowly as if they had the rest of their lives. They kissed and said goodnight.

Tony spent most of the night after he came in from work trying to figure out what Mrs. Davis had in mind. He was sure that she was planning something, and he was sure that he wasn't going to like it. He was confused because he liked and respected Mrs. Davis. He felt that she even liked him. Tony could understand her being upset at him, maybe disappointed, but whatever she was planning, he was not changing his mind.

Tony was anxious to tell Marie about his experience with Dee's mother. Since he was living alone and responsible for himself, he would not tell his mother, Mrs. Peck. He felt that she wouldn't have anything helpful to contribute. His mother, like Mrs. Davis, was a hard-working single parent trying to raise the three remaining children at home. He felt that his mother never understood him, plus he was angry because she had lied to him about his father, and he was not about to forgive her. She never agreed with him or supported him on any issue that he could remember. Although he was the youngest boy, he always went to see her and gave her what little money he could to help out, but he found it difficult to borrow from her when he was broke. It really upset him that his older brothers could get anything from his mother without a fuss, but not Tony.

He lay remembering the incident that led to him leaving home in June, six months before his fifteenth birthday. A neighborhood girl, who was Tony's age, was always coming to visit his sisters, in fact, she was really trying to connect with Tony, but he was not interested. He was in his room trying to study, but Josephine kept interrupting him. After he had had enough, he warned her that if she came into his room again, he would remove her panties. He didn't realize at the time that his warning was what she wanted. Needless to say, she did not heed his warning. When she entered the room again, Tony threw her on the bed and proceeded to try to remove her panties. As luck would have it, Mrs. Peck came home early to find him trying to deliver on his warning. Although Josephine pleaded with his mother, insisting that it was all her fault, Mrs. Peck wasn't having it. She gave Tony some options that he felt were unfair, and he decided to move out on his own. There had been times he regretted his decision, but he refused to go back home. He was alone and afraid most of the time because he felt there was no one he could really depend on except Marie and Dee. He was determined not to go crawling back to his mother. He wanted to make it on his own.

The night seemed longer than usual. Tony sprang out of bed, got dressed, and headed for Marie's house.

"Morning, Tony, come in. You're just in time."

"How's brother-in-law these days, Sis?"

"He's doing fine. They are pretty busy at the station these days. Giving you a week off has him working every other day from six to nine. By the way, he told me to tell you that you will be closing Saturday. We are going to St Louis for the weekend."

"Oh my God, Sis! Does it have to be this weekend?"

"I'm afraid so. We have been planning this trip for a long time. Why, what's so special about this weekend?"

"Well, Mrs. Davis, Dee, and I are supposed to talk this weekend, Saturday afternoon."

"Try to change it, Tony," Marie requested. "We are going to visit some of Clettis's relatives, and we can't change plans at this late date. Anyway, you said that you and Dee were going to talk. You didn't say anything about her mother."

Tony, feeling disappointed, said, "It's a long story, Sis, and I don't have time to explain it now. I will tell you later. Dee and I have decided to get married and get our baby back. I am not sure, but I think Mrs. Davis is going to try to change our minds."

"Maybe she is right, Tony. One thing is for sure, it certainly can't hurt to discuss it."

"Yeah, maybe you're right," he responded in a rather dejected manner.

"Boy, my little brother, married with two mouths to feed before he turns eighteen. You are going to be an old man while your friends are enjoying their youth. Does the thought of that kind of responsibility scare you?"

For the first time, the thought and the responsibility of marriage began to look like a reality, and for the first time, Tony was really frightened.

"Well, Sis, I have to go," he said, his voice shaking as he rose to his feet.

"You hardly touched your food. Did I upset you? I am sorry, Tony, but it's such a big step, marriage and a child."

Peter was the last stop before picking up Dee.

He opened the door and got into the car. "Maxie, why aren't you up here in heaven instead of being back there with those losers?"

Rosey, looking as if he had had a rough night, was in a bad mood. "Peter, could we have some peace and quiet this morning?"

"Yeah, Peter, for once, don't start this morning. Everyone seems to be in a bad mood," Scott said, supporting Rosey's suggestion.

However, Peter was not to be denied. "That's too bad, I am in a good mood," stated Peter with emphasis.

"Peter, it's not that I want to sit back here, but I am being replaced by Dee."

After Maxie shared her reason for change, the car was dead silent for a while, before Peter started laughing and stamping his feet. "Peck, man, I have to give you credit, you don't give up, do you?"

In a very serious tone, Tony calmly stated, "Listen up, Dee and I are getting married. I will probably be quitting school soon."

"Are you serious?" asked Rosey.

"Yes, I am dead serious."

The news took everyone by surprise, especially Peter. "Marriage! Man, that's big stuff."

Recovering from his surprise, Peter injected a little humor. "Well, that means with Tony out of circulation, there will be more for me." Laughing again, Peter continued, "I wish all of you dudes would get married; there would be less competition."

Peter continued at a nonstop pace until Tony left the car to meet Dee at her door.

Upon returning, Peter asked, "Say, mister, why don't you come to our door to pick us up? If we are not running to the car after one blow of the horn, we are left behind. What is this special treatment?"

Everyone was laughing including Dee.

"Good morning, Miss Davis," offered Rosey.

"And congratulations," continued Scott.

Peter explained to Dee, "Mr. Peck told us the news. Say, Tony, can I kiss the bride?"

"Yeah, that's a great idea, Peter," chimed Scott and Rosey.

Peter was trying to put his arms around Dee's shoulder before Tony grabbed it. "No, you all cannot kiss the bride, but Peter, you can lose an arm."

"I don't want to kiss the bride," stated Maxie as she closed her eyes and puckered her lips in a mischievous manner, "but I would like to kiss the groom."

The entire car erupted in laughter except Dee. "You can't kiss the groom, Maxie, but then again, maybe you have already." Dee's comments stopped the laughter, and the remainder of the trip was filled with small talk and occasional silence. Everyone knew that Tony was jealous of Dee, but Dee's reaction to Maxie was unexpected. Although Dee was Tony's girl, the group's allegiance was with Maxie. Dee was seen as an outsider.

Tony quit the football team, foregoing a full scholarship. He got very upset because it seemed everyone in the entire school wanted to know why. On his way home after school, he told Dee why he couldn't meet with her mother Saturday afternoon. Dee didn't seem to be upset about the news.

"Honey, we have to talk. I mean, really talk."

She could sense the urgency in his voice.

"Okay, Tony, when do you want to talk?"

"Tomorrow, let's not go to school. We're going to quit anyway so what's one more day?"

"Tony, I don't know about quitting school, but I will stay at home tomorrow. What time are you coming over?"

"What time does your mother leave for work?"

"She leaves at nine. Why don't you come about ten?"

Tony called to explain his work situation to Mrs. Davis. "That's perfectly alright, Tony. We will talk the next time you come over."

"Thank you, Mrs. Davis."

Tony arrived at ten o'clock sharp the next morning. Dee answered the door wrapped in an embroidered full-length night gown. He had interrupted her shower and she was dripping wet. The gown clung to her magnificent body, and Tony thought he had never seen her as exciting or desirable as she was at that very moment. It was if he had noticed for the first time how much woman she really was. She was pleased to see the excitement in his eyes as she led him by the hand into the living room. He sat as she stood between his knees. Although the nightgown provided some covering, the part that was left uncovered exploded in Tony's imagination. One of her nipples protruded through a small opening, and he remembered thinking that it was the sexiest sight he had ever seen.

They embraced, touched, and explored for hours. He knew at this moment that he would never forget this day. They loved and made love as if there was no tomorrow. Their passion and desire seemed endless. Time had lost all meaning.

"Tony, it's almost three. Ted will be home soon. Help me get things in order."

"Okay, but where do we start?"

"What happened to our talk? We are going to talk, aren't we?" she asked with a grin.

"Yes, Dee, we are going to talk as soon as we get the house straightened out."

They finished with the house and started their talk, and within ten minutes, the door opened.

"Ted, is that you?" yelled Dee.

Mrs. Davis appeared in the door of the living room looking surprised. She didn't say anything as she turned and headed for her room. Dee and Tony were caught off guard by her early arrival, and they both recognized that she was upset about what she saw.

Mrs. Davis reentered the room, looking at Tony. "So you didn't go to school either." Turning her attention to Dee, she said, "Now I understand why you didn't feel so well this morning. You two had this all planned, didn't you?"

"Yes, Mother, we did," Dee replied.

"You two are really amazing. You have brought a child into this world, and you're acting as if nothing happened. You are up to your old tricks. Don't you see how serious this matter is?"

As she talked, Tony wasn't sure if Mrs. Davis was more hurt and disappointed than angry; whereas, he felt she had every right to be angry, her being disappointed made him feel sick inside.

"Don't you realize the same thing could happen again?"

"Mrs. Davis, we won't let it happen again, and we are getting married soon anyway; also we plan on doing something about our child."

Mrs. Davis wasn't finished with Tony. "Does it make you feel like a big man to have a child?" she asked with fire in her eyes.

Tony shot back, "No, it doesn't make me feel big. It makes me feel bad."

"Are you sure, Tony? After all, you have something to brag about with the boys," snapped Mrs. Davis.

"Mother, he isn't like that and you know it. What's wrong? We are trying to do the right thing. What more do you want?" Dee asked almost in tears.

"Mrs. Davis, why did you keep Dee away from me when she was pregnant? Why wouldn't you let her see me?" Tony asked, trying to hold back his tears as he spoke. "You had no right to hurt us like that. You had no right to make us give our baby away."

"Dee is my daughter. I have every right to do whatever I think is best for her. Furthermore, don't talk to me about 'rights' because it is you who don't have any. And don't you get smart with me," demanded Mrs. Davis.

"Please, Mother, we are supposed to talk. Can we talk calmly without fighting," begged Dee.

"Okay, let's talk," retorted Mrs. Davis. "First of all, you kids don't have a chance. There is too much against you. You will end up hating and blaming each other. You both need an education to make it, to have any kind of a chance. You will learn, and it is hard for you to believe right now, but love is not enough. There is much more to a successful relationship.

"If you kids insist on getting married now, I won't try to stop you. If you are getting married for the child, remember, that the child will have a better chance if you allow it to be adopted by a family who can give it the proper home. My suggestion is that you two get back in school and stay in school. Strive to make something of yourselves, and then, if you decide to get married, life will be in your favor. If you love each other as much as you say you do, why not wait? What do you think, Tony?"

"Well, I don't know much about these things, Mrs. Davis. What you say makes sense, but I don't know. I do know that I love Dee, and that I want to make her happy. What do you think, Dee?" asked Tony.

"Tony, whatever you do is okay, but I don't want you to quit school. You still may be able to get your scholarship."

"Okay, we both will go back to school," he resolved looking for approval from Dee.

Tony left Dee's house that day feeling very strange knowing that what had happened was the exact thing that he said would not happen. He was somewhat relieved and yet depressed because he felt an immediate distance come between Dee and himself. The things they had planned, marriage and the baby, were gone. He had been derailed. He was not sure of her feelings anymore. He felt the same but what about her? Had he let her down? Mrs. Davis had won. Marie had won.

The relationship between Tony and Dee had changed. Although they were still close, something was missing. As much as he thought about it, he couldn't figure out what was not in sync. Dee and Tony were acting like an old married couple. Several of their friends and classmates had left school for various reasons. Tony had seen a couple of the guys, and they had changed so much that he hardly recognized who they were. He noticed that the spark in their eyes and their attitudes had gone. Jim, a classmate since elementary school, urged Tony to stay in school. He shared the depth of his soul with Tony. Jim felt that he and Christina had done the right thing by getting married. They both had jobs, and as he stated, they both missed the carefree life without so much responsibility. He urged Tony not to sacrifice his future and that of Dee for a few moments of passion and pleasure. As much as he was troubled by the current situation, Tony felt a deep sense of appreciation for Mrs. Davis and Marie. He realized that they were trying to save him and Dee.

Shortly afterwards, Dee came by the station to wait for Tony on a Sunday afternoon. Several of the neighborhood guys dropped by to get a closer look at the strange girl sitting in the office. Joe, unlike the others, decided to hang around. He and a few others decided that they would keep her company while Tony worked. Dee and Tony had made plans to go to dinner and a movie. While passing the station on her way to the store nearby, Joe called Margo to the office where he introduced her to Dee, making sure he mentioned that Dee and Tony were getting married. Margo was livid but maintained her composure for a while.

"So you are the Dee I've been hearing so much about," Margo said with an attitude.

"Yes, I am Dee. It's funny, Tony never mentioned you," Dee replied, being very cool. "How long have you known him, or maybe I should ask, how well do you know him?"

As he listened, Tony appeared unusually calm, as if he didn't care.

Margo took charge. "Joe, why don't you and Dee come to the house with me? Tony is too busy to keep you company."

"Okay, let's go," Joe was encouraging Dee. "Come on, Dee, Tony won't mind. Like Margo said, he is busy anyway."

Joe was enjoying the fact that Margo and Dee had met. He was the very best at being an instigator, and he was certain to take advantage of the situation.

"Tony, I will be back soon. I am going with Margo and Joe."

Tony wished that Dee would stay with him, but since he was busy, he didn't want to stop her.

After a couple of hours, he had finished two cars, and he wondered what was keeping them so long. In a few minutes, they were walking back to the station. Tony kept waiting for them to come into the office, but when he went to find out where they were, they were heading for Joe's car. He saw Margo and Dee enter the car with Dee in the middle. Joe, about five years older and fifty pounds bigger than Tony, stuck his head in the door where Tony was working.

"We'll see you later," he yelled.

"Wait a minute," Tony yelled back. "What do you mean you will see me later?"

He rushed to the car where Dee was sitting. "Dee, could I see you inside?"

In a glance, he could tell that something was terribly wrong.

"Tony, it was a mistake coming here to see you, a real big mistake! You lied to me, and I will never forgive you. Don't call, come by, or pick me up anymore. I don't want to see you again."

Her words were like a shot to his heart. He tried to reason with her, "Hey, can we talk? You don't know what you're saying. What did I do?"

He did not finish trying to explain before Margo rolled up the window and locked the door, all with a sly grin.

Margo had gotten even as she had promised. She was back dating Melvin, and Dee had been seen with Joe. All of the drama had left Tony feeling defeated. *What a weekend,* he thought to himself, but this morning, he was in no hurry to go to school. Peter could hardly wait to share the news.

"Good morning, all," shouted Peter, looking at Tony. "How's married life?" he laughed. "Say, my man, you'd better watch it, your old lady was seen with this cat named Joe."

"Peter, you are skating on real thin ice," warned Tony. "For what it's worth, Dee and I are finished."

"Don't get me wrong, TP," he said, using Tony's initials. "I don't mean any harm. I just thought you should know. Anyway, what happened?"

"Peter, you are the nosiest person in the world. It's none of your business. Leave Tony alone," urged Maxie.

CHAPTER

VI

Days went by without any contact between Tony and Dee other than passing at a distance. He was hurt and angered by Dee's behavior, not giving him the opportunity to explain whatever Margo and Joe had told her. He knew that he still loved her, but he only felt contempt for Margo. He knew that he could never feel good about Margo again.

The coach refused to let him back on the team with only two games remaining which was a sure indication that his scholarship opportunity was dead. Tony began to escape by burying himself in schoolwork, casual friendships, and hanging out with Scott. Dee continued to be on his mind a lot. The girls he dated all knew about Dee, and for the most part, were threatened. They were all very nice which made Tony feel guilty at times because he knew that with Dee still on his mind, he would not be good for any of them; therefore, he kept everything on a friendship-only basis. There were a couple of older girls that he liked, but he was afraid to pursue them because they liked older men. No matter what he did or who he dated, it was always back to Dee.

Margo finally came around, very apologetic. He had wondered how long it would take her. There were times he thought he could see her shadow in the window looking his way.

"Tony, do you hate me?"

"No, let's forget it," he lied calmly. "It's over and done with."

"Could we talk sometimes?" she asked.

"I doubt it because we don't have anything to talk about."

"Listen, Tony, I said I was sorry. What more can I do?"

"Margo, there is nothing you can do for me, nothing," he emphasized.

In the days to follow, Margo tried every possible way to win Tony's favor, but he rejected her every effort. She would hang around talking to Rob and Clettis, hoping for a chance to talk with Tony, but he always went out of his way to avoid her. Rob had some idea why Tony was avoiding Margo, but he apparently had not shared the information with Clettis. They both saw her as an angel. Although they asked for details several times, Tony never gave any explanation or information. His life was mostly private. He did not call or see Marie much anymore. He felt really alone, and a little scared.

It was a cold, crisp Sunday afternoon in November. Work had been unusually slow. Marie had called to ask him to drop by for dinner. When business was slow, Rob and Clettis didn't mind him closing early. He was anxious to see and talk with Marie, but he was just as anxious to eat her cooking. As he began closing, Wanda, who was a freshman in college, stopped for gas.

"Looks like I got here just in time."

"That's right, I was just closing, but you are always on time with me," he welcomed her.

Wanda was older, more experienced, and more mature than Tony and the girls he had dated.

"Is that so," she said. "Fill it up, I'll be inside," she added, as she hurried inside out of the cold.

When he went inside, he found her in the second bay.

"Wanda, are you lost?"

"I guess so; I was looking for the little girls' room."

"It's around the corner," Tony said, pointing in the direction.

She came back up front, paid, and asked, "Can I warm up in here while you close? The heater in the car isn't working so well."

"Sure, I don't mind it all." He took readings, brought in the products, and counted the cash.

"Are you finished?"

"That's it," he replied cheerfully. "All I have to do is get the lights. Wait here; I'll be right back."

He went to the far bay where all of the switches were located and turned off the lights, unaware that she was close behind him. When he turned around, they were face to face.

"Are you afraid to be in the dark with me?"

Taken completely by surprise, Tony responded, "Should I be?"

She interrupted his comments with a soft, teasing kiss. "Maybe."

"Wanda, what are you doing?"

"Whatever you want to do, but we must hurry," she answered, crushing her full ripe lips against his. *Wow! She can really kiss*, he thought to himself.

Later, he learned that she also knew how to do other things really well. "Whatever I want to do?" he asked trying to control his excitement.

"Yes." Tony quickly led her into a nearby storeroom where they spent the next thirty minutes experiencing everything their passion would allow.

It was a quick burst of passion that Tony needed and enjoyed immensely. Wanda was known for being fast, spoiled, and always having her way. Now, he understood why she always had her way. She was simply great!

"Tony, do you remember a long time ago we kissed, and I told a friend of Dee's, knowing it would get back to her?"

"Yes, but today, you more than made up for any trouble you may have caused."

"This time," she said, "it's only between us, you and me."

"Wanda, Dee and I are not seeing each other. We busted up a while back."

"You are too nice for her. Did you know that when my brother was home from the navy, he made it with her the very first night at the drive-in? I knew you were still together then. Tony, I am sorry if this hurts you, but she really doesn't deserve you."

"Wanda, why are you telling me all of these things?"

"Because I like you; you are a nice guy."

Although he wasn't sure why she told him about Dee and her brother, he didn't think she was trying to hurt him. He liked her as well.

"Well, Tony, I have to hurry. Mom will be driving me back to school later today."

They said their goodbyes, and he headed for Marie's.

"What's happening, Tony? No one sees much of you these days. Are you okay?" she quizzed before he completely entered the door.

"Sis, no one can ask as many questions as you. Now, what question do you want me to answer first?"

They both laughed. Most of the family was there for dinner. Some of his family he hadn't seen for a few months. It was not a close family. Mrs. Peck, his mother, was glad to see him. Even though she didn't show it, he knew it. She and Tony had some pretty serious differences. She seldom, if ever, expressed love towards him. Most of all, she was very surprised that he had not returned home after their big disagreement. After leaving that afternoon, he knew that he would never go back home to live.

Most of the family knew Dee personally or knew about her, and as always, several members asked about her. No one knew that they were not seeing each other although he would tell Marie when they were alone. While enjoying the family gathering, Tony was surprised when Marie handed him the phone. He knew it couldn't be Wanda. It was Joe.

"Tony, who do you want, Dee or Margo?"

"Why and who wants to know?" Tony asked, trying to be composed.

"Well, they both like you, and it's not fair because I like Dee and a friend of mine likes Margo."

"Listen, as far as I am concerned, you can have them both. I don't care."

Joe continued to pursue the subject. "You don't want either of them? Is this what I am hearing?"

"Look man, this is a crazy conversation. If you want Dee and she wants you, go for it. As for Margo, you both can have her, I really don't care."

Tony had been hoping for an opportunity to catch Joe at a disadvantage. This little confrontation made him feel good. Tony rejoined the family. The gathering was nice, and he was happy to see the family interact in such a calm and peaceful manner. All too often, these gatherings would produce serious disagreements or worse.

As much as he enjoyed the family and the dinner, Tony wanted everyone to leave so that he could have Marie to himself. Clettis would always give them space. It was like he knew that Marie was the only person Tony could talk with about his situations. Shortly after the phone rang, Marie gave him the phone, and again, he excused himself to their bedroom.

"Say, man, you don't know me. I am a friend of Joe's, but did you say that you didn't want Dee or Margo?"

"Whoever you are, I don't know you, and I have said all I have to say." Tony, not so gently placed the phone in its cradle.

After everyone left and Clettis went to bed, he told Marie everything. At first, she was worried, but the more they talked, she realized how well he was handling it all.

"Tony," she exclaimed, "you are too young for all of these crazy things to be happening to you. Are you sure you're okay?"

"I am okay, Sis, don't worry about me. I'll make it through all of this mess," he assured her.

Although he had settled into a routine, he was thinking more and more about Dee. Since football was over for him, he had plenty of time. On many occasions, he arrived at work early which made Rob and Clettis happy because they were always ready to leave when he arrived. Several days had passed since his encounter with Joe. He only saw Dee at a distance, avoiding every possible chance of accidentally running into her, like taking different routes to get to classes.

As he and a friend walked to the parking lot, she broke off the conversation rather abruptly, "Looks like you have company. I will see you later."

Tony was surprised to look up and see Dee waiting beside his car.

"You have a minute?" she asked, looking a little troubled.

Tony noticed that she didn't look so well, like she had been sick or not getting enough sleep.

"Sure, what's up?"

"Did you tell Joe that you didn't want me anymore? Tony, tell me the truth. I need to know," she was looking straight into his eyes, pleading. "All I want to know is did you say it?"

"Yes, I said it. What did you expect me to say when Joe called asking me those kinds of questions? What did you expect me to say?" he responded raising his voice.

"Did you mean it? This is what I really need to know," she persisted.

"Why Dee? Why all of a sudden do you have this need to know how I feel? Since you have shown that you don't give a damn about me, what does it matter whether or not I care for you?" countered Tony.

"Wait a minute! What's this about Joe anyway?" she shouted. "The last time I saw him was the day after I left the station. He calls, but I won't go out with him. Tony, I am not seeing Joe or anyone else. He wanted to know if I refused to see him because of you. When I told him 'yes', he told me what you said. Now do you understand, Mr. Peck?"

"Yes, Miss Davis, I almost understand, but not quite," he said jokingly as they both laughed and made fun of the situation. "Can I give you a ride home?"

"Yes, everyone will be glad to see you. Mother has asked about you several times."

"We had a family dinner at Marie's about a week ago, and everyone wanted to know where you were. I didn't tell anyone that we had stopped seeing each other until Marie and I were alone."

The ride to Dee's house was filled with small talk since they were trying to catch up. Neither Dee nor Tony made any reference to the times they had spent apart.

There was something about this time together that he had not experienced before, a kind of peace. There was more concern and gentleness in their voices and in their manner. Tony was particularly impressed that Dee had not been dating, which was not the case in past breakups. Margo had been the only serious encounter he'd had since meeting Dee. Things were not only back to normal, things were better than normal between him and the entire Davis family. The joking, playing, and laughter among him, Jan, and Eli were like old times. Ted was usually in the vicinity jumping and turning flips as kids will do. Delores and Tony begin to talk more. She was rather quiet and serious, but friendly. Tony thought she was very attractive.

Things were going very well for Dee and Tony. They began to spend more time with the family. The urgency and need to be alone had somehow diminished although they had their time alone. Their sex and lovemaking was less frequent although their passion and desire for each other remained constant. They began to behave like an old married couple. Through Thanksgiving and Christmas, their lives continued to be filled with love, peace, and tranquility.

In January, everyone started talking about future plans, going to college, getting a job, or getting married. Although Dee and Tony had never mentioned marriage since they talked about quitting school, it was assumed by family, friends, and everyone else that they would be married. Dee and Tony had never shared their plans for the future. They talked of love and being together for the rest of their lives, but they never made specific plans.

It became final, Tony lost his scholarship. He became moody and distant towards everyone, including Dee. He knew that he could not afford to pay his way through college. The thought of working in factories and foundries was not appealing to him at all. He was also well aware that he could not live on what he was making at the service station. All of a sudden, he thought, life was really beginning to get scary, reminding him of how heavy the thought of marriage and family weighed on him a few months past. He knew he would have to leave the city, but where would he go? What would he do? What about him and Dee?

CHAPTER

VII

By late January, Margo really began to go downhill. Tony hadn't seen much of her, but when he did, he noticed a distinct change. She looked much older, beaten, and drained. She had lost weight. Rob had asked about her, saying that she had stopped coming over, and that he never saw her anymore. He wanted to know if she had gone back home. Margo's sister, Ellen, was also worried. Ellen came by after Rob and Clettis had left.

"Tony, it's none of my business, but what happened between you and Margo?"

"Nothing really, we just drifted apart, that's all. Did you ask her?"

"Phil and I tried to talk with her," Ellen explained with a worried expression. "But she has been impossible lately. We are worried about her. She refuses to find a job. She sleeps all day and stays out all night. Tony, I know you've seen her. And I know she still likes you. Will you please talk with her? Please?" Ellen pleaded.

"I don't know, Ellen, what makes you think she will listen to me?"

"Maybe she won't, Tony, but please try."

Ellen paid for her soda and left with the understanding that he would talk with Margo.

Ellen and Phil had always liked Tony. He didn't like the assignment he had accepted, but he too was concerned about

Margo. She was deteriorating right before his eyes, and he had felt nothing until approached by Ellen. She and Phil had been married about a year. Ellen had been married to someone else shortly before marrying Phil. The word on her was that she was "hell on wheels," that she played around. Tony never talked about anyone, but he was exposed to most of the gossip. He always thought that people were jealous of Phil, an average guy, for having a woman that was way above average. Ellen and Margo were the most attractive and desirable women on the south side, and the most talked about.

Almost a week passed before Margo came by the station.

"How have you been, Tony?" she asked in a serious and subdued manner.

"I've been okay. What about yourself?"

"Don't play games with me, Tony. Look at me," she requested. He looked.

"I am a mess. Do you have to ask how I've been? By the way, how is Dee? She is a nice girl, Tony. I hope you will forgive me for what I did to you. I am very sorry," her eyes filled with tears. He embraced her and comforted her without either of them saying a word for a moment.

"Come on, Margo, don't cry," he begged trying to hold back his tears. "Listen, I'll forgive you if you promise me something." He was holding her at arms' length, looking into her eyes. "Will you promise?"

"Okay, I promise," she agreed reluctantly. "What is the promise you want from me, Tony?"

"I want you to promise that you will stop hurting yourself, and that you will go back to being the girl that everybody liked, respected, and admired."

She thought for awhile with a sad look on her face. "I don't know, Tony. You ask a lot. I'll let you know, okay? One question: do you care what happens to me?"

Tony knew that there was only one answer. "Yes, it's very important."

She was pleased with his response. "See you later," she said as she left.

A couple of days passed before Margo returned, looking much better, and in a good mood. "You got your promise, but if I don't find a job soon, I am going back home."

"I hope you find a job. By the way, you look great, and yes, I do forgive you."

She was all smiles when she left. He was sincere when he complimented her on how good she looked, but he lied in wishing her success in finding a job because he could tell that she wanted more than a job and certainly more than he was willing to give. His life was in order, and he didn't want her trying to create problems. He and Dee were very happy.

He had not been at the station five minutes before the phone rang. It was Margo.

"I am just calling to say goodbye. I will be leaving tomorrow."

Tony looked across the street to see her waving from Ellen's bedroom window.

"Thanks for calling. Are you happy about going home?"

"No," she emphasized. "But, I guess it's the best thing to do. One last favor, Tony, could you take me to the drive-in to get something to eat after you close?"

She never gives up, he thought to himself.

"Okay, I have a little time, but I can't stay long because I have a lot of homework."

"Thanks, Tony, it won't take long. I'll be ready."

Tony was hoping that Margo's hunger for food was genuine, but he wouldn't be at all surprised if it wasn't. He had standing permission to close up to an hour early when business was slow, and on this night, he decided business was slow. He wanted to close early so that he could take Margo to the drive-in and be home for Dee's call around ten thirty. After he finished closing, he left his car at the station while he walked across the street to get Margo. He didn't want to park in front of her house. With Joe and his friends living in the neighborhood, Dee would have the information before he got home.

As he walked across the street, he noticed that the garage was empty, which meant that either Ellen or Phil, or both, were not at home. The thought of returning to his car was powerful, but he continued. Margo answered the door clad only in a robe.

"Tony, you are early. I thought I had another thirty or forty minutes. As you can see, I just stepped out of the shower."

At this time, Tony wanted to kick himself for not telling her that he would be early. He had created this situation.

"Yes, I am early, but I thought you'd be already dressed. Anyway, you don't have to go through all of this just to go to a drive-in. How long is it going to take you to get ready?"

"Not long," she called from her bedroom. "But we have to wait for Ellen and Phil. Junior is in bed asleep, and I can't leave him alone. They won't be long."

Tony was getting anxious. The phone rang.

"Tony, get the phone," she yelled, still in her bedroom.

Ellen sounded surprised to hear Tony's voice. "Tony, is that you?" she asked hesitantly.

"Yes, it's me," he responded.

"Tell Margo that Phil and I will not be finished for another couple of hours."

It was the worst news he could have received.

How was he going to get out of this situation without a hassle? Margo was still in her room.

"Who was on the phone?"

"It was Ellen. She told me to tell you that she wouldn't be home for another couple of hours."

She was silent for a moment. "Come here a minute, Tony," she requested.

"What do you want? You come out here," he shouted towards the room.

"If we don't stop all of this yelling, we're going to awaken Junior. It's not like you've never been in my bedroom before. Come on," she urged. "Are you afraid of me?"

"No, I am not afraid of you, but since we are not going to the drive-in, I need to get going. I have homework." He lied about not being afraid.

"Are you sure Dee isn't waiting?" she teased.

"Don't start on me, Margo," he warned.

"Okay, okay, don't be so touchy. Sit down and relax. Don't forget, this is my last night," she said, as she grabbed him gently by the arm with one hand guiding him to the side of the bed and closed the bedroom door with the other. When the door was closed, he knew that he would not be at home in time to receive Dee's call.

Tony wasn't sure how much of what was happening had been planned, but he knew it was too late to run. Margo was as charming, desirable, and seductive as ever. He knew that he shouldn't be here with her, and for a brief moment, he felt a pang of guilt which disappeared almost as quickly as it had appeared. Avoiding her had been relatively easy, but resisting her now, he thought, was impossible.

"Tony, could we forget all of the bad things that have happened between us and focus only on the good things," she purred as she snuggled up close. "Let's make this a very special night. After all, we may never see each again. I will remember this night, and I am going to make damn sure you do, too," she offered convincingly while removing her robe.

He had almost forgotten how stunningly beautiful she was without clothes and the heights of passion and desire she could arouse within him. Soon, it was as if it was their first time to make love and to explore each other as they shared and gave as if indeed this would be their last time. They lay spent, savoring the moment. Their lips were one, their bodies one, both sealed in ecstatic bliss.

"I will never forget you. I have never felt all of the things I feel when I am with you. It's going to be difficult moving forward. Do you think you will miss me just a little?" she whispered.

"You know I will miss you. Don't forget the promise you made."

They shared a tender farewell. As he walked to his car, he felt relieved.

On the way to his room, Tony remembered that Margo had been there when he needed someone. Their last night together had nothing to do with love, for he knew that he would always love Dee. Although being with Margo was wonderful in a strange, inexplicable way, he was relieved that it would not happen again even if she stayed. He felt that he owed Margo a 'last night'. After all, she had helped him when he was hurting.

Winter turned to spring as life moved on without much of a hitch. Tony had become well adjusted to the routine of school, work, and school. On his time off, he and Dee began spending more time together. In many ways, he felt that their love had grown stronger, more intense, more settled. They seemed to depend more on each other as each day passed. They looked forward to the time they had together and dreaded the time away from each other. Their lovemaking became a daily occurrence, or at least, with every opportunity. They appeared to be obsessed with being close, touching, embracing, and expressing a love and desire that seemed to intensify with each spoken word. Casual glances were rare between them because they looked at each other with such wanton desire that even a stranger could paint their thoughts. Dee and Tony held each other's hands with the will and determination of maintaining life support. They were inseparable indeed.

Although he liked and admired other girls, Dee had been his one and only love. Margo came close, but she was long gone. Tony thought very little about her, but he wished her well. There was a lot of talk about the new girl on the west side. Everyone was talking about her, even on the south side. Tony was curious to see what all of the fuss was about. He was sure Peter would be able to bring him up to date. The ride to school was quiet until Peter got into the car.

"Tony, my man," Peter commented a little excited. "Are you coming to the 'Place' tonight?"

"I don't know. I work until nine."

Peter was still excited. "Man, you don't want to miss tonight because Maxie is brining the new chick. Man, she is fine."

Looking at the excitement in Peter's manner, he was already trying to think of how to explain it to Dee because he knew someone would tell her.

"Peter, I don't know. Dee would be mad as hell if she knew I was out."

Peter became a little perturbed. "Dee! Man, you ain't married to her, and she is not your mama. Peck, the talk is that you two are too tight. You two don't give each other any breathing room. I couldn't handle it."

"Peter, you know I don't care what 'the word' is. Dee and I are tight and I like it; furthermore, I don't need anyone's permission to go any place. I will see you about ten, and this new girl had better be worth it."

Shortly before closing, he tried to call Dee, but she wasn't at home. Normally, he would be upset since she didn't call. He wondered why she didn't call. Anyway, he decided her not being at home provided the perfect opportunity for him to join Peter.

When he arrived, the parking lot was packed. Tony was excited about the evening as he rushed inside. Once inside, he saw Peter sitting with some friends from the south side which was somewhat surprising since the west and south sides were usually at each other's throats, mostly over girls. On his way to join Peter, he was intercepted by Eddie.

"Hey, Tony, I knew you couldn't be far behind. Dee and Dorothy left about twenty minutes ago."

"Thanks, Eddie, are you sure she was with Dorothy?"

He was sure. Dee knew Tony didn't like Dorothy. Dorothy's boyfriend was part of the group that hung around the station talking about girls, and Dorothy was trying to set Dee up with one of her boyfriend's buddies. Tony had no respect for any of the group that hung around the station.

Tony quickly forgot the upsetting bit of information.

"Tony, over here," Peter yelled, standing to get Tony's attention.

Before he could sit down, Peter wanted him to meet the new girl. "Man, this place is really hopping," he said, excited as usual, at the same time taking Tony by the arm, leading him to where Maxie was sitting with a very beautiful older girl. As they approached the table, Maxie got up and pulled up another chair.

"Betty, this is Tony. You met Peter earlier. The girl you met, named Dee, is Tony's sweetheart."

"Please to meet you, Betty," he said, taking her hand and looking into her eyes.

"So you're already taken, I hear, Tony? Why does your girlfriend let you run around loose?" she teased.

Maxie was not impressed. "Save your breath, honey, he has a one-track mind; it's called Dee."

Tony was a little embarrassed. "Come on, Maxie, how do you know?"

Peter was enjoying the play among Betty, Maxie, and Tony. He was a different person in a crowd; whereas, Tony was more alive and outgoing. They talked, danced, and passed the time. Tony and Betty changed seats to be close so they could talk. After a while, they spent most of their time just talking to each other. Everyone noticed. Already some of the other girls hated her, and many of the guys hated Tony. Betty and Tony were very cozy until Rosey came to whisper in Tony's ear that Dee had returned and was headed in his direction.

Betty had heard. "I guess your girlfriend has returned. This means you will probably have to go, but I am sure we will see each other again."

"Don't count on it," countered Maxie.

"Be cool, Maxie. I will see you tomorrow," Tony warned, not understanding Maxie's attitude towards Betty.

By this time, Dee was standing behind his chair. "You must have finished work early, Mr. Peck?" she asked sarcastically.

"Yes, I did. I called, but you were out," he answered, getting up from the table. "I'll see you all later. Nice meeting you, Betty."

Dee was not happy with what she had seen. As he stood up to face her, she stared him straight in the eyes. "I want to see you outside, now," she demanded.

On their way to the door, Tony heard voices from the crowd saying, "I am available, Dee."

"Give him hell, Dee."

"Let's see you explain your way out of this, Mr. Peck."

"You finally caught him, Dee."

He was wondering why these people, most he didn't even recognize, were harassing him. Dee walked ahead of him to the car, and he could tell that she was pretty upset.

Once inside the car, she asked, "Were you going to take her home? What would have happened if I hadn't returned? Why the hell were you spending so much time with her anyway? I had been watching, and I just wanted to see what you were going to do. Looks like I almost waited too long."

Tony didn't like being on the defensive, "Where have you been? You weren't home when I called, and you weren't here, where were you?"

"I was with Dorothy and her boyfriend. We went by your place and when you didn't come home, we decided to come back here. We saw your car outside so they dropped me off, and boy, I am glad they did."

"Honey, I don't know why you are so upset, I didn't do anything," he reassured her.

They traveled to his room in silence. When they reached the privacy of his room, alone, they forgot the rest of the world. Putting his arms around her waist from behind, kissing her neck and ear, he said, "Dee, I am sorry. You know that I am yours. I don't want or need anyone accept you."

"I am not so sure," she said half jokingly, "but I don't want you to see that girl again."

She turned to face him as they embraced and engaged in a passionate, lingering kiss. Their kisses were strong and penetrating, burning. She abruptly broke away from his kiss.

"No, not tonight, Tony. Don't you ever get enough?"

"Why do we have to stop, it's just you and me?" he asked in an urgent state of passion.

"I know it's just us, but I don't want to, I don't feel like it. Can't we enjoy each other just once without going all the way." Dee was becoming agitated.

"Let's not do it tomorrow, but right now I want you very much. I'm hurting, please, Dee," he continued to plead.

She was sitting on the side of the bed straightening her blouse. "No, Tony! I want to go home," she demanded.

"Dee, how can you leave me like this?"

"If you don't take me home right now, I'll take the bus."

"Honey, it's after twelve, the buses have stopped," he smiled.

Being unable to change her mind, Tony took Dee home. She was angry about the attention he gave Betty and he was frustrated. In the car, she tried to hold his hand, and he refused which heightened the tension.

Dee became inflamed. "So if I don't screw you, you don't want me to touch you? Is that the way it is?"

"No, that's not it and you know it."

"Well, if all you want is a 'screw', you'd better go someplace else."

She was more upset than he had ever seen her. Tony was beginning to think that maybe it was more than seeing him talk with another girl.

"Look, Dee, I said okay, and I am taking you home, what is the problem? But if you want me to go to someone else, I will."

In an instant, Dee lashed out, striking Tony across the face. The blow momentarily blinded him as he pulled the car to a stop in the middle of the street hoping to avoid an accident. Enraged by her blow, he jumped out of the car, ran around to her side, opened the door, and grabbed her by the arm to get her out of the car. While attempting to pull her out of the car, he saw the fear in her eyes, and all he wanted to do was to alleviate the look he saw in her eyes, to console and reassure her. Once out of the car, he held her.

"Darling, you know I didn't mean what I just said. I don't want anyone but you. I am sorry, Dee. Please forgive me?"

They stood motionless for awhile just holding each other. She pulled away just enough to see his face.

"Are you okay?" she asked with tears. "Did I hurt you? Honey, I didn't mean to hit you. It just happened, I couldn't help it," she was touching and kissing his face where she had landed the blow.

They ended the night with love and affection. After taking Dee home, he had a little time alone to reflect on what had happened. What had he planned on doing to her after she struck him? The thought of ever striking her made him nauseous. He would not be like his father. The thought was unbearable.

Peter could hardly wait to tell everyone the latest episode in the lives of Tony and Dee. Tony thought he would never let up. His exaggerations were hilarious, even Tony had to laugh. Since he was not participating in sports, the group usually rode to and from school with him, and almost always, the trips were lively and fun-filled. Time was passing quickly; just a couple more months, and school would be over. Most of the group were concerned about their next step except Scott and Rosey. They knew exactly what they were going to do, which college they would be attending. The pressure and apprehension about the future were sometimes frightening for Tony. He often thought about his future with Dee, but never made any real plans. Dee had been accepted to a college up north. Since losing his scholarship, his future was mostly uncertain.

A month or more had passed since Dee had struck him, and he had kept his promise not to see Betty although it was very difficult because she would call and make herself available, but he never accepted. Tony had been trying to call Dee for a couple of hours. Although he had left a message, he decided to try one final time. Jan answered the phone.

"Jan, this is Tony. Is Dee home yet?"

Her reply shocked Tony. "She was never away from home. She is in the driveway sitting in some guy's car."

Holding back his anger, he said, "When she comes inside, tell her to call me."

He picked up his keys and ran to the car. As he approached the driveway, he could see the car, but the windows were steamed, making it impossible to see inside. Not being able to see inside, Tony approached the car and opened the door. The sight of her close to someone else was devastating.

"What the hell are you doing, Dee?" he shouted.

"Close the damn door," the voice inside the car demanded.

"I can't believe this," he shouted as he slammed the door and headed inside.

As he headed inside, he was trying to hold back the tears, hurting as he had never been hurt before. Mrs. Davis tried to console him, but he was very agitated. When he looked through the window, the car was gone. He went to the door expecting Dee to be coming inside with an explanation. Soon, he realized that she was still in the car. He was frantic.

"How could she do this to me? How could she?" he asked, as he paced and looked through the window for Dee.

Eli and Jan were surprised to see Tony this way. He was always so cool. They also tried to calm him.

"Tony, calm down, it's nothing," Jan spoke while trying to hold his hand. "She doesn't like him, Tony."

"Don't worry, I am sure she will be right back," offered Eli.

Mrs. Davis was very calm. "I told her to get in here, but of course, she didn't listen. You have a right to be angry Tony, but I'm sure she will be back soon. Just sit and wait, and in the meantime, try to be calm. You may not agree, but it's not the end of the world." Mrs. Davis left the room after giving Tony a reassuring pat on the back.

It was the longest five or ten-minute wait of his life before he heard and saw the car in the driveway, heard Dee's footsteps leading to the front door, and saw her enter the room where he, Jan, and Eli waited. He wasn't prepared however for what followed. Dee entered, slamming the door behind her, and rushed to where Tony was standing, and looked him straight in the eyes.

"Who gave you the right to spy on me?" she screamed as she turned and ran to her room, slamming and locking the door.

Tony was completely dumbfounded at her behavior. He still expected an apology or at least an explanation. He tried to catch her before she locked the door, but she was too quick.

Realizing that he had to control himself in the company of her family, he tried to reason with her.

"Dee, come out here. I want to talk with you," he knocked and talked through the door several times without receiving any response from Dee. He enlisted the services of Mrs. Davis. "Mrs. Davis, could you please ask Dee to come out so we can talk?"

"You kids know I don't like to get involved in your squabbles," Mrs. Davis said somewhat annoyed. "Dee!" she shouted. "Get out here now!"

Dee still refused to respond. At this time, Mrs. Davis approached him in a consoling tone, "Tony, maybe you two should try to talk about it tomorrow. Let it go for now, okay?"

"Yes, ma'am, but why is she refusing to talk to me? I haven't done anything to her." He noticed Jan and Eli watching. He had almost forgotten where he was. Although he felt an urgency to talk with her tonight, he knew it would not be wise to go against Mrs. Davis's suggestion. "I am going, Dee. See you in the morning."

Her response made him weak with pain. "Don't bother picking me up in the morning, and don't ever call either," she shouted through the door. Her words were like a bolt of lightning and as penetrating as a knife to the heart. He left without another word, too hurt and bewildered to speak.

What a night! he thought to himself. He and Dee had had many situations during their five years together, but he felt that this one was the "back-breaker". After all they had been through, this hurt the most because he thought everything was fine. Would he ever be able to trust her again? Tony found it impossible to sleep. He got up early. He needed to see his sister. He needed someone to listen to his heartache.

He rang the doorbell twice and waited before Marie answered. Since Clettis didn't have to be at work until noon, they had decided to sleep late.

"Did I wake you up, Sis?" he asked.

"That's okay, I was about to get up anyway," she lied. "This is a surprise." Marie yawned, trying to wake up.

"Sis, I caught Dee with someone else last night, and can you believe, she refused to talk about it? She even accused me of spying on her. Sis, I love her, but I have just about had it with her. Don't you think I deserve an explanation," he asked, looking for approval.

"What do you mean, you caught her? What was she doing? Anyway, it does appear that she owes you an explanation, but I am only hearing your side of the story, and you know how I feel about taking sides. You and Dee will have to work this out between the two of you. I can imagine how you must feel."

"You don't understand, Sis, she won't ride to school with me anymore, and she told me not to call. I am the one who should be mad."

Marie had never seen Tony look and act so helpless and worried. She was very concerned about him, but she too felt helpless because he wasn't listening to any of her words. She faced him, putting both her hands on his shoulders while gently shaking him. "Tony, please listen to me. Sometimes people who love each other hurt each other the most, and sometimes the hearts can be mended and sometimes they can't, but there is one thing for sure, life goes on no matter who is hurting. You are much too young to be so wrapped up and miserable over one girl," she continued in a tone he had never heard before. "You have a couple of immediate choices. You can ignore her wishes and try to pick her up, hoping that you two will be able to talk things out, or you can respect her wishes and hope that she will call, which I recommend you do. Either choice can hurt. Tony, just because you love somebody, it doesn't mean that person has to or will love you back. There aren't any guarantees when it comes to relationships. I really wish I could help. Honey, please try to move on," she said, taking both of his hands in hers.

"Thanks for the advice, Sis; it does help. Say hello to Clettis. See you later, and thanks again."

On his way to pick up Scott, he decided that he would go by to pick up Dee anyway. He and Scott talked about baseball, the prom, and going to college. Scott was a brain; he had received an academic scholarship plus his dad had left him funds for college. After leaving Peter's house, Tony proceeded on to get Dee. As he came closer to the house, he became more anxious. He felt that she would go with him, but if she didn't, the embarrassment and pain would be overwhelming. The thought of her rejecting him in front of the group was especially frightening because he knew Peter would have a field day at his expense.

As he approached the front door, his heart was pounding, and his knees were shaking so that he had to support himself with a chair.

Dee was waiting at the door. "Why are you here? I told you not to pick me up, I have a ride," she spoke in a cold, unfeeling tone, closing the door before Tony could speak. Tony returned to the car more angry than hurt this time, but before he could back out, a car pulled in behind him.

"Where is Dee?" asked Peter. "For awhile, I thought you were leaving without her."

"I was," Tony replied. "She wasn't ready so we will go on without her," he lied.

He was looking back trying to get the car to move when Rosey interrupted, "She looks ready to me, but how are we going to get three more people in this car?"

Before Rosey finished, Tony looked around to see Dee, Jan, and Eli walking past his car to get into the one behind him. The group all turned around to look, amazed. They all looked at Tony as the other car backed out and headed up the street.

Tony found it impossible to hide his feelings.

As expected, Peter, the comedian, was the first to speak. "Did anybody see what I just saw? Man, you want to tell us why your ol' lady is riding with another dude? I mean, if it ain't asking too much; after all, we are your friends," teased Peter.

Maxie said, with a forced smile, "Peter, shut up. How would you feel?"

"Damn," moaned a dumbfounded Scott. "That is too much."

"What are you going to do, Tony?" asked Rosey.

"I am not going to do anything. This is it, we are definitely finished. I hope I never see that bitch again," Tony spoke with all of the venom and defiance he could muster.

The rest of the ride to school was filled with a lot of small talk. The group was trying hard not to acknowledge what had just happened. Even Peter didn't feel comfortable making jokes. They all appeared to have compassion for Tony in his time of hurting.

This time, he was determined to move on without Dee. He began to date other girls but stayed away from any girl that he might be able to take seriously. On weekends, he spent more time at the recreational center where most of the guys and girls his age could be found. Peter was always on the scene trying to teach Tony the 'ropes'. Peter even offered him a drink and a smoke on occasion, but he always refused. Within a few weeks, he had dated several girls and thought very little about Dee. Getting serious was not something he wanted to do, and he always made it clear with whomever he dated.

It was like he was just beginning to live, to experience the kind of life he knew existed, but had never tried because of Dee. Renting a room in a place that only rents to single women had its advantages. He had always avoided the women in the building where he lived because of the advice given by the doctor's wife who pressured the doctor into renting him a room. He didn't want to disappoint Mrs. Jefferson. Since he and Dee were history, he spent more time in his room. He usually left his door open and many of the women would come in and talk. He was always invited to dinner, or just to visit. It wasn't long before he began socializing more and more with several of the women to the dismay of their men friends.

Tony's life was going at a fast pace and so was time. He still had no plans for a job or college. Most of the time, when he thought about the future, he became almost paralyzed with fear and uncertainty. Otherwise, he enjoyed his increased popularity at home as well as other places. He had always been one of the best dressed and groomed among his peers, and he was seldom found without money.

CHAPTER

VIII

School was coming to a close; the end was just a few months away. Freshmen and sophomores could hardly wait for summer, juniors were anxious to get to their final year, and seniors were apprehensive about what lay ahead. To soothe some of their anxiety, seniors had the prom to keep their minds on less stress-provoking matters. Many were determined to make it a night to remember.

With all of the talk about the prom, Tony hadn't given it much thought.

"Tony, who are you taking to the prom?" asked Rhodes, one of Tony's more affluent friends. When Tony was short on money, he could always count on Rhodes.

"Don't know yet, haven't decided. Who are you guys taking?" he asked, referring to Rhodes and Tom.

"Listen, Tony, we have a great idea for the prom, or should I say, after the prom. My family has a couple of cabins on the lake in Wisconsin, and we are thinking about leaving right after the prom. It's about a two-hour drive, and we can stay the entire weekend. What do you think, Tony?" asked Tom.

"What do I think?" Tony responded showing a great deal of excitement. "Wow! The idea sounds great, count me in," replied Tony still trying to hold back the excitement.

Watching him, Rhodes and Tom became excited, putting their arms around Tony. "One thing, Tony," whispered Tom. "We must keep this a secret. Only the girls and we three are to know about this little getaway."

"Fine with me," Tony promised as they parted. Tony was one of the more respected kids in school, and there was no way he would divulge their secret.

For the next few days, he was overflowing with joy. He was one of the few black kids who was liked equally well by whites and blacks, including his teachers, with one exception. He briefly dated his music teacher. He found the experience to be very friendly and very pleasant. Although they stopped dating, they remained very close, but kept their distance.

The things that Tony had taken for granted the last three years were about to come to an end. He was frightfully close to entering the adult world. He knew that he would miss school, the acquaintances, his teachers, and friends. As difficult as it had been at times in his personal life, he knew that he would sometimes long for the relatively simple life of the crowded halls and brief conversations between classes. It seemed to him that he had already spent more time in the adult world than his peers, and he feared the bottomless pit of adult problems.

The rides to school were filled with after-graduation talk. Although everyone appeared to be looking forward to that final date with some degree of bliss, there was obvious apprehension. All of a sudden, the group seemed to have grown up without warning. Even Peter had become more serious.

"TP, my man, I need a big favor after school if you're not too busy?" asked Peter in his usual jive fashion.

"You need a favor? Remember, I don't loan money or my best girl. We can negotiate everything else. Now, what is the favor you need, Mr. Cook?" teased Tony.

"I need to go downtown to the army recruiting office to take some tests," responded a more serious Peter. "I've decided to go into the army. The job scene doesn't look worth a damn around here, and I don't have college cash so I've decided to give 'Uncle Sugar' a try."

Tony was taken aback by Peter's plan. "Gee wiz, man, the army, you, Peter Cook? I don't believe it."

"If I go now, my obligation will be finished by the time I am twenty-one. Maybe by then, I will know exactly what I want to do. What are your plans, Tony?" asked Peter.

Tony pondered the question for a while. "I don't know, Peter. See you after school." The conversation between Peter and Tony occurred as if they had been alone. None of the others participated; they just sat and listened. Tony was surprised.

It was very difficult for Tony trying to picture Peter in the army. Now, it appeared that everyone had a plan except him. He was sitting in the hallway at the post office waiting for Peter when he was approached by a marine.

"Are you being helped?"

"I am here with a friend; he is going into the army," Tony answered.

"The army?!" exclaimed the marine jokingly. "The marines got a better deal. The army is a bore."

Tony and the marine laughed hardily.

"Roy, I heard you," shouted someone from the army office. "Stop trying to steal my people. I always knew you guys were hard up."

Everybody in both offices were joking and having fun. Tony was impressed.

He knew about the marines. A friend had dropped out of school in his junior year to join the marines. He had shared many of his experiences with Tony, and he had absolutely no desire to become a part of what he had heard.

"What is the test about?" Tony asked the army man.

"Well, there ain't much to it," he was told. "Would you like to take it?"

"NO, NO," emphasized Tony by raising his hands.

The army man was quite persistent. "Why not? You don't have to sign any papers, and you don't have to join. Why don't you take the test just to see how well you can do?"

The marine yelled, "Now who is stealing? I asked him first."

"It's not first that counts, it's who's the best," the army man bragged.

Tony took the test to Peter's surprise. He and Peter didn't talk about the tests or the army. Their conversation was mostly about girls and the good times.

"Peck, I have to say, you have really gotten loose since you and Dee busted up. Do you think you two will ever get back together again? Everybody is really surprised that you two haven't gotten back together."

Tony was surprised that he had thought so little of her lately and that he could pass her and speak to her in the halls without going crazy. As Peter continued to talk and ask questions, Tony began to feel some of the anger and hostility he felt towards Dee because of the break up.

"Man, you get tired of taking a person's shit. If I had deserved it, it wouldn't have hurt so damn much, but I did nothing to deserve her shit, and as far as I am concerned, we will never go back together. I've had it with her."

While Tony was talking, Peter was looking at him in a manner of disbelief.

"Peter, what's your problem?" Tony snapped.

"Be honest, Tony, you still love her, don't you? Come on, tell the truth," he urged jokingly while poking Tony in the side.

"Stop it, fool!" Tony shouted, trying not to laugh. "Okay! You know I don't like to be tickled so stop it! Let's talk about something else if you don't mind?" asked Tony, becoming a little agitated.

That evening, Tony talked with Rob and Clettis about the army since they both had served. They thought it may be a good idea since he wasn't going to college. Clettis had received several wounds in Korea. With each passing day, he thought more and more about the army and leaving Dee behind. He began to wish the weekends away so that he could see her at school. He decided that if he didn't see her in school, he would seek out Eli to find out how she was doing. Eli was a sophomore in the same school, but he and Tony's paths seldom, if ever, crossed. He was determined to find Eli.

"Eli," waved Tony.

Eli waited and appeared to be glad to see him. "How's it going?"

As usual, he was friendly and happy to see Tony. "Great, Tony, don't see much of you anymore. Just because you and Dee broke up, you don't have to stop coming around."

"Well, Eli, it's like this, I don't want to make Dee's new boyfriend angry, or cause any problems for Dee, you understand," Tony explained, hoping to get information on Dee's situation.

"Oh, she wouldn't mind at all, and I am sure that she doesn't have another boyfriend. So you see, it's okay."

Eli's information made Tony feel like jumping for joy. He wondered why she didn't have anyone, why she didn't date. *Surely, she must have heard about my activities*, he thought to himself.

Prom time was a little more than two weeks away. Both Rhodes and Tom wanted to know who he would be taking. Tony knew who they were taking.

"Fellas, I don't know for sure yet, but you know I will have someone."

"Okay, Tony, but remember, you can only take one," Tom said jokingly.

They all laughed. Many of the guys envied Tony for his success with girls. Several parents had tried to steer him towards their daughters, but there had always been Dee. He was liked by most of the girls and some of the guys. Many adults were impressed that he worked and was a good athlete and an honor student, but only a very few people knew he lived alone and supported himself. Tony was careful not to give out his number or where he lived, not even Peter knew his living situation. He always gave Marie's phone number. He was known by the girls as the perfect gentleman. He was seen as more mature than his peers. He never talked or gossiped about anything or anybody.

Working at the station, he heard all of the rumors and gossip. He always remembered the only good advice his deceased father ever gave: "A relationship with the opposite sex is private, never share it with anyone." It was good advice that Tony had followed. Because of rumors and gossip, he knew many secrets about the lives of many people.

Since he was not seeing Dee anymore, Tony spent more time in his room. After work, he usually went to his room. He had just arrived from work in the hallway on the way to his room when he heard someone call his name. It was Ruby. She lived on the same floor. Ruby was about twenty-seven and petite, but attractive. She had invited Tony into her place several times, but he always had an excuse. Her door was cracked. When Tony knocked, she answered the door with a drink in her hands, in a very good mood. He could hardly take his eyes away from her body as she was rather scantily dressed, certainly not in her usual white nursing uniform. As he entered the room, she came closer, her scent was simply captivating.

"A lot of homework tonight?" she teased almost in a whisper.

"No, not really," he replied taking a step backward.

Tony had admired and desired older women from a distance, but there was always something about older women that frightened him.

Several of the women had invited him to their apartments, and sometimes, he went; especially if dinner was included. Tony loved to eat, and he had been accused of being willing to do anything for a good meal. Some of the women had made hints, but none as strong as Ruby. Although he liked Ruby and was excited, he found himself a little frightened. He had always heard that older women were better at everything. Older women, he was told, were givers, not takers like girls his age, plus they knew what they wanted, and how to take care of themselves. They didn't get pregnant.

"Well, then, there is no reason why you can't keep me company for awhile, is there?" she asked.

Tony felt trapped. Before he could answer, one of the motherly types walked by her door. "Child, you should be ashamed of yourself," she said while passing the door.

Closing the door, Ruby completely ignored her. "Come on, Tony," she urged. "I won't bite. You don't have to stay very long; I know you have homework to do." She took his hand and led him to her bedroom.

Once inside her bedroom, Tony noticed how nice and orderly everything was; he was impressed. She left the room for a while and returned with a drink. "Here is a soda. I've heard that you don't drink or smoke, but I'll bet you have a lot of girlfriends, don't you?" she teased.

"No, not really," he said, still nervous, his voice trembling.

"Tony, is this the first time you've been alone with a woman in her apartment?" she asked, sensing his discomfort.

"No, not really, but this is different, I guess."

She was moving closer. "What do you mean this is different? Don't you like me?" She was very close.

"Yes, I like you, but..."

She interrupted, "But what, Tony?"

He was intoxicated with the smell of her perfume and very excited by her body touching his. She felt his excitement, "Do you want me?" She was hardly finished speaking before he grabbed her. "Wait, slow down, we have all night if you want," she whispered, trying to slow his passion.

Almost immediately, he began to accept the truth about older women, for each whisper, each kiss, and each touch or move seemed more exciting. She said and did things Tony had never experienced, things that he was sure to want again.

As their passion raced to unbelievable heights, she took control. "No, not yet. Let's make it last forever." Her body was completely still, but her hands and her lips continued to fuel the fire he felt inside. He had lost all sense of time. Ruby had given him an experience he had not known, yet there was no love, just lust, passion. He thought to himself out loud, "Who needs love when you can feel this good without it and all of its problems?"

After they had consumed each other, Tony lay quietly with Ruby in his arms. "Ruby, you are wonderful, and I am very glad you invited me."

She smiled, looking very pleased. "Are you sure you're only eighteen?" she asked, placing a playful kiss on his forehead.

"I'd better go. It's after midnight already."

As he attempted to pull away, he noticed that she had fallen asleep.

"I am sorry I went to sleep on you. What are you doing? Where are you going?" she quizzed, trying to keep him from getting up. "You don't have to go, Tony. Can't we just stay like this the rest of the night?"

"Okay, but I have to get up at six."

They spent the night in each other's embrace. The excitement was so intense that Tony was only able to sleep for short periods of time. His restlessness also made it impossible for Ruby to sleep.

"You are not sleeping well, are you?" she asked.

"No, I can't seem to relax. It will probably be a long day because I will have to get up in about three hours."

She turned to face him and realized that he was still excited. "Poor baby, you still want me, don't you?" she sighed, pressing her body tightly against him.

"Yes, very much, very, very, much," he whispered.

This time their lovemaking was much more vigorous, more passionate, completely unrestrained, and out of control. Their passion peaked as their bodies shook violently from the simultaneous explosion within. Drained and fulfilled, they drifted off into a deep sleep.

"Ruby! Ruby!" he shouted while shaking her. "Wake up. It's after seven. I am really late."

Tony sprang out of bed, dressed quickly, and dashed down the hall to his room. He called Peter, Scott, Rosey, and Maxie telling them to catch the bus. While in the shower, he briefly reflected on his time with Ruby, and he shouted out loud, "Oh, what a night!"

Since he didn't have any detours, Tony arrived at school about the same time as usual. As he came within sight of his locker, he saw Dee standing there waiting on him. Immediately, he felt a twinge of guilt.

"I tried to call you last night, but I couldn't find you anywhere. Where were you, Tony?" she asked.

"Good morning, Dee. Where are your manners? Don't you speak anymore?" he asked trying to make light of her concern while he fumbled through his locker.

"Tony, I don't want to upset you. I just wanted to know that you were all right," she explained.

"Well, as you can see, I am doing fine, but why the concern all of a sudden?" he asked still annoyed. "If you are concerned, you have a hell of a way of showing it. You haven't passed up an opportunity to rub my nose in shit since we've known each other, so don't give me this business about being concerned," he snapped and walked away. As he turned the corner, she was still standing beside his locker.

Later during the day, Tony was confronted by Charlotte, the comedian, a friend of Dee's.

"Tony, you're a jackass. It's not going to hurt you to be nice to Dee, and don't tell me that you don't know that she still loves you," Charlotte scolded.

"Charlotte, do you know why we broke up? Dee may be your friend, but she is far from being an angel. Anyway, it's none of your business. I don't want to talk about it."

Charlotte was on the heavy side, very smart, and aggressive. She always got her way. "Listen, Mr. Smartass, your business ain't no big secret, and just in case no one bothered to tell you, your halo has turned to horns," she continued, not giving Tony an opportunity to speak. "It won't hurt to talk with her. I'll tell her you will see her after school." Again, she kept him from responding by walking away.

Although his thoughts were mostly filled with Dee, he found the time to think about Ruby. He had no idea what would happen with the talk he had been bullied into having with Dee. Tony wasn't even sure he wanted to talk. All of a sudden, he realized that he was afraid of Dee. Loving her had caused so many heartaches, but somehow, he knew that he would be there to talk with her. He was always there, and she knew it. The thought of her always getting things her way, on her terms, infuriated Tony. He decided that he was not going to be so easy anymore. In the next to the last class, he saw Dee and beckoned for her.

"Dee, I can't see you after school."

She made no attempt to hide her disappointment. "I had looked forward to us having a talk. Are we ever going to talk?" She looked as if she wanted to cry.

"Yes, I will come by tonight after work."

He was surprised and delighted to see her eyes smile with his offer to see her.

"I will be waiting, Tony."

CHAPTER

IX

Things were moving quickly for Tony, and he felt that he had little or no control over any of it. The prom, graduation, the future, and Dee all weighed heavily on his mind. He pondered a future with and without Dee and was equally frightened by both.

On the way home, Peter asked about the prom. "You going to the prom, ain't you, mister?" he asked.

Tony knew that any time Peter used the word "mister", he was in a good mood.

"Yep, I guess so, but I don't have a date yet. What about you? Who are you taking?" asked Tony since he never heard Peter mention anyone on a consistent basis.

"Elizabeth! Peck, where have you been? Everybody knows she is my woman. Oh, I hear Bill asked Dee, so if you are planning on taking her, you'd better get moving." Peter was giving both information and a suggestion, but most of all, he was interested in Tony's response. "By the way, I thought you had heard about Bill pursuing Dee. The word is that you two are talking again so I guess you got everything covered."

Looking at Peter in disbelief, he said, "I swear, Peter. Who are these people that tell you everything? Yes, we had a few words today, but we are not back together."

They rode in silence for a short while before Peter made one of his profound statements. "I say it's only a matter of time before you two are an item, and when that happens, you are going to have to stay out of the streets," he chuckled.

After work, Tony rushed to see Dee. All of the family was glad to see him, and it felt good, he had missed them. He and Dee made small talk as if they were trying to find their way to a more serious conversation. Tony was not in a very patient mood.

"You know I am still mad at you for what happened the last time I was here. I haven't been able to forget it, and I don't know if I will ever forget. Why did you do it?"

Dee had never seen Tony so assertive and to the point. "I don't know, Tony. I don't know why it has taken me so long to say 'I am sorry' because I was sorry the minute I saw you hurting. It's just that I really didn't think you cared anymore. I thought you just wanted to 'make out' with me. Sometimes I didn't feel that I was good enough for you with you being so much in demand. Everybody talks about you, and all of the girls seem to want to be with you. Tony, I just couldn't see how you could love me as much as you said. When we decided to give up the baby and not get married, I felt that I would lose you for sure," Dee continued explaining through her tears. "I guess you could say I am always crying."

He sat there on the couch beside her trying to match her words and expressions, and maybe for the first time, he was beginning to understand her. "Come on, let's go for a walk," he suggested while wiping away her tears.

As they were leaving her porch, he turned a couple of steps below her so that they could look each other in the face. They stood for several minutes talking about the love and need for each other, and how they would never stop loving each other. They walked hand in hand just enjoying being together until the rain came, then sought shelter under a big tree where they embraced.

"You know what I want to do, Tony?" she asked with a child's mischief in her eyes. "I want us to walk in the rain, and I want you to kiss me until we are soaking wet."

He looked at her with a big smile. "Anything you want darling." He liked seeing her so happy. Tony and Dee walked hand in hand, stopping to kiss after almost every step. After a while, they were running and playing in the rain like children.

Dee started riding with the group again. Her mood changed when he told her that he might join the army, but she promised to wait and write. She became all smiles when he told her about spending a weekend in Wisconsin after the prom and asked her to go with him.

"We will have to talk with Mother. She would kill both of us if we just took off without her permission. Will you ask her with me? There will be others going, right?"

"Yes, Rhodes, Tom, and their dates, but you must keep this a secret. No one else can know our plans, okay?"

She agreed. He usually left by eleven, but Dee wanted him to stay longer tonight.

"Honey, I'd better go, or your mother will ask me to leave soon."

She finally relented. "Tony, one last question, will you be dating other girls?"

"Dee, I have never dated anyone while we were together, and I never will," he promised.

She smiled. On the way home, he thought about all of the things Dee had said, the things that bothered her, and he vowed to himself that it would never happen again.

Everyone was talking about Peter and Liz. Before, only Tony had a steady, now it seemed the entire group had a special sweetheart. Everyone had prom dates. Maxie had moved to the back seat with Dee on board. With everyone on board, Tony headed in the in the direction of Dee's house.

"Looks like we will have an extra person this morning," commented Peter, everyone laughed, including Tony. "Oh well, it's no more than I expected. I am only surprised it took so long."

The group wanted to hear about Peter and Liz.

"Peter," interrupted Rosey, "we've heard enough about Dee and Tony. I hear you and Liz had a little problem at the Center over the weekend. Do you want to enlighten us or shall I repeat what I heard?"

The entire car cheered.

"Yeah, Peter, tell us all about it," continued Scott. "You are good at telling on others; now let's hear what you have to say for yourself."

Peter, turning to face Maxie, said, "I know you're behind this." Trying to hold back his laughter, he said, "You all have been dying to get something on me. Now you've got it, but it's not a big deal, I am still in charge." The ride was filled with uproarious badgering, fueled mostly by Maxie.

Dee was standing outside waiting, looking very special.

"My, my," exclaimed Peter. "Look at Miss Dee, ain't she cute?!"

There were times when Peter's mannerisms were more comical than his comments. Everyone was laughing and acting a little crazy when Dee entered the car. It was one of those mornings when everything was funny.

"Dee, you will have to excuse us. This is just one of those rare days," explained Scott.

"It's okay, but will someone tell me what is so funny," Dee asked with a curious smile. Although not knowing what was going on, Dee got caught up in the fun and laughter, which pleased Tony greatly because in the past, she always appeared to be a little uncomfortable.

Tony explained about Liz and Peter.

"Don't tell me Peter has a sweetheart," Dee stated in disbelief. "I thought you were too busy playing the field to settle for one girl, Peter."

Maxie laughed at Dee's comment. "Peter playing the field? Maybe that's what he wants you all to believe, but I know better. He's lucky if he has one."

The laughter was deafening. Tony thought that this was the most fun the group had ever had on their way to school, and he was happy that Dee had joined in.

A few days had passed since he had talked to Ruby. Dee was coming over on the weekend, and he wanted to let her know. A knock on Ruby's door produced a man in a housecoat.

"What do you want?" he asked in a not so friendly tone with the door half opened. His presence caught Tony by surprise.

"Could I speak with Ruby? My name is Tony. I live down the hall."

He could hear Ruby's voice as she neared the door behind the gentleman.

"Tony, it's good to see you. Where have you been? Come in." She took the door away from the man and reached out to Tony.

Realizing that he had come at a bad time, he tried to refuse her offer to visit. "No, no, that's okay, I will come back later. I am very sorry to bother you. Anyway, I just wanted to say 'hi'."

Ruby was very persistent. "Oh, come on in here. I want you to meet someone."

As he was led into the room for an introduction, Tony could feel the hostility from her friend. "Tony, meet Andy. Andy, this is Tony, he is sort of the man about the house."

Andy remained seated but extended his hand. "Nice to meet you, Tony. Tell me, how does it feel to have all of these women fighting over you?"

Tony wasn't sure if Andy was being funny or sarcastic. "I really don't know because I am at work or school more than I am here," explained Tony.

"Well, young man, you don't have to look in on Ruby. I'll be around to look after her so you will have plenty of time for some of the others."

Ruby appeared to be surprised and disappointed with Andy's words and behavior, but she never said a word.

He said his goodbyes to Ruby and her friend. Instead of going directly to his room, he stood in the hallway for a while to hear part of the argument he was sure would happen. It was obvious to Tony that Ruby's man friend didn't want him in her apartment. Under the circumstances, Tony didn't feel that he needed to explain Dee's upcoming visit. Although Ruby was very attractive and exciting, Tony was glad that she belonged to someone else.

Rhodes and Tom had arranged for the girls to answer the phone in one of the cabins and the guys in the other. This way, the girls could say that they were going with other girls which would be more acceptable to their parents. Tony had mentioned the idea to Dee, but she preferred telling her mother the truth. They both agreed to discuss it with Mrs. Davis over the weekend. Mrs. Davis had been very good to them considering all they had put her through, and Tony didn't want to take any unnecessary chances of creating new problems. He liked the idea that the girls were going together. What if they asked Mrs. Davis and she said 'no'? The guys, including Tony, were more excited about the weekend getaway than they were about the prom. They were also glad that Tony was taking Dee because everyone knew and trusted each other.

Dee was waiting with excitement and a beautiful smile when Tony arrived after work. They decided to go to the lake in the park, but decided to leave immediately after sunset to go to his room where they could be alone.

"Dee, I've been thinking about telling your mother that we are going to Wisconsin together. Honey, I really feel that it would upset her, and to be honest, I don't want to upset your mother anymore. Please tell her that you are going with the girls. She may even know that we are going to be together, but actually telling her that we are going to be sleeping together for three or four days is something else altogether. What do you think?" Tony asked hoping that his argument was convincing.

She was sitting across the room facing him; he was sitting on the side of the bed. She stood up and walked towards him with a calculating grin. "What do you mean sleeping together?" she asked, as she jumped on top of him, pushing him backwards across the bed. "Do you mean like this?" she continued to play and try to maneuver his body in different positions. He had only seen Dee in such a mood twice during their relationship, and he knew that it meant that she was extremely happy. He remembered this time, like before, he didn't quite know to what extent she was kidding.

"Dee, stop messing around," he pleaded. "This is serious. I really want to know what you think," he moaned.

"You're no fun at all," she pouted. She stood up and started to pace around in the room as if she was trying to think, much of the time fighting the urge to burst into laughter.

Tony was puzzled and defeated. "Okay, Dee, you win. I can tell you're not going to be serious so let's talk about something else."

She stopped pacing and looked at him, still smiling. "I agree, my dear," she mused. "That's why I told her that I was going with the girls."

They stared at each other and smiled.

"You teaser! You were putting me on all along. You really had me going," he confessed with a sigh of relief while jumping up to put his arms around her.

She was filled with laughter. "Now that we have that settled, let's talk about the serious stuff, like sleeping together," he teased.

"Tony, what would happen to us if I didn't sleep with you? Would you still want me to go to Wisconsin with you?"

As she asked the question, there was a seriousness about her he had not seen in a while. She stood motionless waiting for an answer. Sensing the importance of her question, he caressed her cheeks in his hands while looking into her eyes.

"Dee, I just want to be with you, and yes, I would want you to go with me even if you didn't kiss me."

It was the answer she wanted. "Okay, Tony, I get the point, but don't overdo it."

They laughed. Dee and Tony had never been happier. Their time together was treasured by both. They spent hours together and hours on the phone. It was if they were 'one'. They laughed and played all evening, and in between, they fused each other's passion with ecstasy so profound that they were paralyzed with sheer delight.

Although he had enjoyed other girls as well as other women, there was something special about Dee that Tony was not able to explain. She was, in his mind, beyond compare. He knew that he would never tire of her because in all of their time together, he had never come close to getting enough of her. Her kiss, her touch, and the way she completely gave herself to him gave him a deep feeling that he had never experienced. Tony was secure in what he knew was a mutual and uniquely special love relationship. "Dee, Dee, wake up," he whispered while caressing her breasts and in between her thighs.

She turned to face him, noticing that he was excited. Half asleep, she responded, "I was going to ask you why you were waking me, but I think I know." She snuggled close, their bodies straining as their lips searched and found heaven with all of its shooting stars. "Tony," she sighed, almost ready to explode, "I want you now. Oh darling, hurry."

Tony was completely absorbed in trying to respond to her heightened urgency. "Yes, honey, I want you, too. I always want you. I don't seem to ever be able to get enough of you."

They expressed their love and delight until the bed came crashing to the floor, but neither seemed to notice until their ultimate fulfillment, then they both laughed uncontrollably. What rapture! What wonder!

As the prom day crept near, so did Tony's date with the army. The two dates were the most important in his immediate future; one would bring a very special event he would share with Dee, and the other would take him away from her. He had mixed feelings about going away as Dee was becoming more a part of his life each day. The thought of leaving her behind left a deep, dull sensation within him.

Rhodes, Tom, and Tony started spending more time together as their big weekend at the cabins drew nearer. They were all excited as were the girls. The guys knew that the girls would keep their secret since they appeared to have more to lose, but they all kept reminding each other of the importance of secrecy.

"Can you imagine what would happen if the word got out about our plans?" asked Tom.

"I don't see how that could happen. Only we three know, and you can bet the girls won't tell. There's nothing to worry about, is there?" offered Rhodes.

"I am already on shaky ground with Dee's mother. If she heard about this, man, it would be over for me. Let me put it like this: if the word gets out before we go, Dee and I will not be going. Anyway, we are not going to tell, and the girls are not going to tell. I agree with Rhodes, there is nothing to worry about," Tony said, directing his statement to Tom.

Every time the guys saw each other and got the chance, some comment about the secret prom weekend was made. There was so much anticipation and excitement centering around the prom week that it became a major distraction for both the girls and the guys.

Peter and Tony would be leaving on the same day for the army. They would be taking the train to Chicago. Tony was still trying to picture Peter in the army. It was still a picture out of focus. They would be leaving one week after graduation. Monday morning came rather quickly. The trips to school had become strained as conversations were becoming increasingly serious.

"I can't believe you guys are going into the army. What do your women say about you leaving?" quizzed Rosey.

"Liz is not too excited about it, but she understands," explained Peter.

"What I want to know," quipped Scott, "is with you two so madly in love, who's going to take care of business while you two are away fighting for your country? Did you think about that fact?"

Scott's comments provided a spark that livened the trip, except for Peter and Tony.

Maxie seemed to enjoy Scott's comments and the discomfort it created in Peter and Tony. Maybe it was because, among the group of four guys, she had no equal. "Oh, don't worry too much about Peter and Tony," she assured Scott. "They are probably like most guys. They expect the girls to stay home and write while they are out messing around all over the world. Well, I hope Dee and Liz will do no more and no less than Peter and Tony."

Her comments drew laughs from Scott and Rosey but no response from Peter and Tony; they just rolled their eyes at each other. Tony was not getting into the trenches with Maxie in this kind of conversation because he couldn't bear the thought of Dee being with anyone else again.

"For your information, Miss Maxie, I will be true to Dee, and I will write her every day," he responded rather sarcastically.

Maxie seemed to be waiting for Peter or Tony to challenge her. "Why should Liz and Dee stay cooped up, writing letters when they could be out having fun? And the same goes for you and Peter. As for me, I don't want a boyfriend if he can't be with me."

Tony expected Peter to challenge some of Maxie's views, but he avoided getting serious. "Listen, I don't know about Tony, but I am not going to worry about what's going on as long as I get my letters. Hey, I am hundreds of miles away; I can't do anything about it, so why worry?" asked Peter.

Before arriving at school, it seemed everyone had given their philosophy on life and love except Dee. Being away from Dee for any part of his three-year commitment weighed heavily on Tony's mind all during the day.

CHAPTER

X

"I am not going to work today. Would you like to go to the park and then to a movie?" Tony asked as they walked hand in hand to study hall. He could always tell what Dee's answer would be when she would squeeze his hand and give him that special look.

"That sounds great," she smiled. "I will fix a couple of sandwiches and we can stop for some sodas. Tony, you always think of such wonderful things."

Mid-May in Northern Illinois was a beautiful time of the year. The grass was green, flowers were in full bloom, and the air was almost intoxicating. He and Dee talked about how pretty this day was. The skies were blue, the sun was bright and warm with a light, gentle breeze. It was the kind of day lovers dreamed about sharing. It was a perfect day for them; they were free, very much in love, and together. They decided to go to a different park. It was busier than their favorite park, but it was closer to the movie. Anyway, once the blanket hit the ground, it would be just the two of them no matter how many people were around.

They lay on the blanket, he on his back, and she lay facing him with her head on his chest. It seemed that every moment was very special, loving, and peaceful.

"Dee, I want you to know that I have been happier the last several weeks than I have been my entire life, and it's all because of you. It is really hard to describe just how happy I am."

Dee looked into his eyes and gave him a very playful but affectionate kiss. "Tony, do you really have to leave? We are so happy now, I don't want it to ever end. I miss you already. What am I going to do without you?" she asked as the tears began to flow.

Previously, she had said very little about him leaving. Like her, Tony was really beginning to dread leaving. "There you go," he teased while holding and consoling her, "getting me wet again. Oh, honey, don't cry," he begged trying to hold back his tears. "We'll be back together before you know it, and I promise to never leave you again. Anyway, I promise to write six times a week."

They talked for awhile before drifting off to sleep. Tony sat up in a rush, trying to remove what he thought was an insect in his ear, but he realized that Dee had been tickling him with a leaf. She was laughing at his reactions. He chased her around, and they wrestled and played on the ground until they were exhausted. They ate, relaxed, and toyed with each other as if each was a prized possession.

They were holding each other close when he asked, "Could we take a quick detour by the apartment before the movie?"

She smiled, knowing exactly what he had in mind. "No, because we'd never get to the movie on time. To be honest, I'd love to, but this isn't a good time." Somehow, the time had slipped away as they had to rush to make the movie on time.

As usual, Dee cried. "I guess you could say I always cry in movies," she joked.

"No, not always, but most of the time," Tony replied, smiling.

"Tony, you are not as tough as you pretend. Sometimes you look as if you want to cry."

"Well, maybe I do, but I don't," he responded. "It's okay if you cry in movies. I don't mind at all," he assured her. The drive to Dee's home was quiet with her sitting very close while he drove.

Tony went inside to say hello to Mrs. Davis and the family. Mrs. Davis was busy in the living room when they arrived. "Tony, I hear you're going into the army right after school."

Dee had apparently told her mother. "Yes, ma'am, I think it's best to get it over. I will be gone for three years, and when I return, I won't have to leave again," he explained.

"Do you know how Dee feels about you leaving?" asked Mrs. Davis.

"Mother," Dee was embarrassed.

"It's amazing," Mrs. Davis continued. "You mean to tell me that you kids are going to stay away from each other for three years, and for the past several weeks, you haven't stayed away from each other three hours," she mused.

"Mother," said Dee. "We have discussed it, and we are going to wait for each other. It will be okay."

Mrs. Davis looked as if she still had a few things to say. She listened and looked at them standing in the middle of the living room holding hands. "You both are very young, and I know you two might think that waiting is an easy thing, but the truth of the matter is that waiting is very difficult no matter how much you love each other. You both will change more in the next three years than you have at any time during your short lives. Just be willing to fight for each other when things get tough because they might," Mrs. Davis advised. After she finished, Mrs. Davis left the room.

Her speech frightened Tony. "Dee, no matter what happens, I am coming back to you," he promised and reassured her.

"When you come back," she promised, "you will find me waiting."

Final exams were right around the corner, scheduled for the Monday after the prom, which created quite an uproar throughout the student body. Fortunately, the student council was able to convince the administration to have exams the week of the prom.

Dee was very excited about the dress she had planned for the prom, and Tony was anxious to see it, but she refused, saying that it was bad luck and that it would spoil the surprise. Dee, at times, looked much more mature than her age. Tony thought that she was the most beautiful girl in the world. He had rented a tuxedo to match her colors. The prom and the cabin all in one weekend had all of the anticipation of something more special than any experience he had ever had, not to mention that it was the next to the last weekend before he would be leaving.

Tony liked school, his many friends and acquaintances, and the hustle and bustle of the hallways. It was difficult for him to explain the many emotions he felt about it all coming to an end. As he looked back, school life had remained the most consistent and stable part of his life. It was a place where he felt appreciated, respected, and needed. He was quite familiar with school life and very comfortable with it, but just as uncertain about life after school.

It always helped to share his anxieties with his big sister, Marie. She seemed to always know when he needed to talk. As always, things were much better after a few minutes with her. He felt very lucky to have such an understanding sister because many of his friends had the same fears but no one to listen.

The days kept moving along at a rapid pace. The weather, from what everyone said, was the best in years. The exceptional weather filled the parks and "lovers' lane". Dee and Tony spent their share of time in both. Parks and lakes were favorite meeting places Saturday evenings and Sunday afternoons. Just as he had begun to see a difference in Dee that he had never seen, he was beginning to see a city and its people for the first time; all of which he had taken for granted for so many years. All in all, life couldn't have been better for Tony, and he and Dee had never been closer. The thought of leaving everything, especially Dee, was very painful, sometimes bringing tears. He knew that once he was away, he would lose all control. Tony felt helpless and bewildered, and the things Mrs. Davis had said about being separated weighed upon him.

The last three weeks of school, Tony left his room to move in with Marie and Clettis until he left for the army. He stopped working to spend more time with Dee and made arrangements to sell his car. His days in the city were numbered, as well as his days with Dee.

With school coming to an end, there were parties everywhere. It was as if some of the celebrations had as much to do with avoiding fears and uncertainties as it did with joy and cheer. Many classmates who had never smoked or drank were beginning to engage in these escapes. Everybody seemed to be doing strange things; it was mostly those without plans. Dee and her family were very happy as she had been accepted by the college of her choice. Before he lost his scholarship, he and Dee had planned on attending the same college. Tony had always heard that education either made people grow closer together or further apart. It was an unsettling thought since he and Dee were going in different directions.

"Don't let those college boys steal you away from me," he joked.

"Tony, I've never been so happy in all my life. No one will ever take your place in my heart. I will be good for you, and I will be true." She continued in a less serious manner, "Just make sure you don't let anyone steal your heart. You know what they say about a girl in every port." Before she had completed her sentence, Tony was rolling in laughter. She looked at him, puzzled. "Mr. Peck, will you please tell me what I said that was so funny?"

He pulled her close, still laughing. "Honey, I am not going into the navy, remember?"

Dee was a little embarrassed. "The army, the navy, what's the difference? You are still going away. Why do guys always leave the girls behind?" she asked in a sad tone.

"You know, Dee, we had it all planned. We were going to be together in college. What happened to those plans?"

Trying to console him, she said, "Now who's getting upset? Let's just enjoy the time we have left, okay?" she begged in a whisper while standing between his legs as he sat on the park bench.

Dee and Tony had been coming to the lake for several evenings to watch the sunset. From where they sat, it appeared that the sun set in the lake.

"Dee, I never knew sitting and watching the sun set could be so special."

She would never take her eyes away from the direction of the sun, always sitting or standing between his legs, never letting go of his hands. Sometimes sitting between his legs with her head leaning back against his shoulder, she would watch the entire sun set without a word, dazed, hypnotized.

As they walked to the car arm in arm, he felt an almost uncontrollable urge to be with her. "You will never guess what's going through my mind," he said.

Her response caught him by surprise. "Whatever it is, let's go to Marie's and discuss it. You did say that they would be away until about ten, didn't you?" As she spoke, she was amused by Tony's reaction to her suggestion.

"Yes, they will be late, but do you know what you are saying?" They were in the car in a flash, hurrying to be alone.

Dee broke the silence to explain her comment which still somewhat baffled Tony. "Tony, we don't have much time before you leave. I know we can't love each other enough to last for the time we are going to be missing and needing each other, but we can make every minute count. I decided last night that I would not deny you anything from now on. Darling, I am yours anytime, anywhere, anyway you want me."

They were being overcome by the need and the passion they had felt many times before. Driving became a major task as they began to touch, search, and explore each other in their rush to seek privacy where their raging passion and desires could be unleashed.

Although surprised by Dee's expression, her openness had created a new bond, an excitement that was new and stimulating. They both rushed from the car to the back door and down to the basement to his bed where heaven awaited them.

The rides to school became more routine and subdued, filled with small talk and petty gossip. The group diverted their attention away from events in each other's lives. It was a change that puzzled Tony. It seemed that the group became more serious each day; they didn't have fun or joke anymore. The ride was not loose. Maybe it was because so much was upon them, the prom in a few days, and exams. Tony thought to himself, *Do people in the 'real' world have fun?* Like it or not the 'real' world was about to arrive.

Over the weekend, Tony decided to visit the doctor and his wife to thank them for renting to him. He also visited some of the women he had gotten to know. Ruby had moved out. He was disappointed because he wanted to see her one last time. Most of the weekend was spent daydreaming about next weekend at the lake. Tony ran into Susan and Becky, Tom and Rhodes's dates for the lake. They were shopping for their trip. They were excited. As usual, they asked about Dee, and wanted to know if she was as excited as they were.

The more Tony thought about going into the army and leaving Dee, the faster time passed. He felt good about the trip to the lake; it was going to be the best possible sendoff. Exams were a breeze since Tony found most of his classes to be rather easy. The group, or more appropriately, Maxie decided that it would be nice to have a celebration after exams to recognize the group that had been riding together for the past couple of years. She, Dee, Tony, Scott, Rosey, and Peter headed for the park immediately after class. It really was a special gathering, a sentimental farewell although a week of school was still ahead, but it was just one day before the prom.

All of the talk the next day was related to the prom. It was prom-time. With exams behind, it seemed that every ounce of energy was now directed towards the evening. The trip to school was filled with a quiet excitement, a silent scream. Everyone seemed more loose and relaxed.

"Can you imagine having to take exams Monday after the prom," moaned Peter.

Everyone talked about sending a 'thank you' note to the student council for their insight.

Scott, the intellectual among the group, said, "Well, one thing is for sure, the grades will be better."

Everyone laughed in agreement.

"Scott, is that all you think about, grades?" exclaimed Rosey. "We are talking fun."

"Don't worry about these dummies, Scott," countered Maxie. "Just think of them when you make your first million. You are right, the grades will be better. Exams on a Monday, after the prom, was a dumb idea."

"All I know is that I would have found it very difficult to study for exams this weekend," joked Tony.

"Let's face it," Maxie shouted trying to get a word in with everyone talking at the same time. "Scott is the only person in this car that is serious about school."

"Maxie, you are going to make somebody a good wife. Not only will you tell him everything he ever wanted to know, you will also tell him how, what, and when to think. Girl, you don't know everything, do you?" Rosey's comments were funny to everyone except Maxie.

After the laughter, they all waited for Maxie to crush Rosey, but she never said anything accept to give him a look that could kill. For once, Maxie let someone else have the last word.

After arriving at school, Dee and Tony sat in the car for a while.

"Are you all packed and ready to go, Dee?"

"I am all packed, but I can't put my things in your car or Mother will suspect that we are going together. What are we going to do, Tony?"

Sensing her concern, he said, "I know what you mean. Tom and Becky have the same problem, so here is what we decided to do. After the prom, we are going to take all of you home to change. Susan and Becky will come by to get you, and we will all meet someplace. Get ready as quickly as you can because they will be there. Susan will know where to meet us. How does that sound?"

Dee gave him a big smile. "It sounds great. How long did it take you guys to come up with this idea?"

They both laughed and joked, looking forward to the evening.

"Man, I can hardly wait to see the prettiest girl at the prom. Be ready, I definitely will not be late," he commented as they parted.

Tony had to meet Tom and Rhodes too before class to solidify their plans. He had lied to Dee because the guys had never made detailed plans, but what he told Dee sounded great. As he approached Tom, he noticed a worried look on Tom's face.

"Tony, we've got a big problem. I can't pick up Becky, and her mother insists that she come home before leaving for the weekend. Any ideas? What about you and Dee?"

Tom was pretty worked up over the situation. As usual, Rhodes and Susan didn't have a problem. They had been seeing each other since eighth grade, like Tony and Dee. Since they were engaged and expected to marry within a few months, their parents didn't place any restrictions on their activities.

Tony shared the lie he had told Dee. They all thought about it briefly before Tom exclaimed, "By golly, it's perfect. Rhodes, can Susan pick up Dee and Becky?"

Rhodes didn't see any problem with the plan. "Hold on guys," he said, as they were about to part. "We haven't decided on a meeting place," reminded Rhodes. "And Tom, you will have to give me a ride to the meeting place because I can't ride with Susan."

Everyone agreed on a place to meet, and the worried look on Tom's face had disappeared. While everyone else saw the prom as the highlight of the year, Tom, Rhodes, and Tony were anxious for the prom to be over.

Tony walked around in a daze the remainder of the day, not remembering anyone or any event, accept the times he saw Dee between classes. The small talk continued among associates and friends, mostly about the prom and the future. As days rushed by, for many, the effects or anticipation of the final curtain being drawn became more intense. The many friends and relationships were quickly coming to an end as many would never see one another or share again. It took all of his energy to fight the urge to become melancholy when thinking about the army and Dee. Tony just wanted to think about the evening and the weekend.

CHAPTER

XI

After putting the final touches on his tuxedo, Tony put the rest of his weekend clothes in the car and rushed to get Dee. The moment had finally arrived, and it was difficult for him to manage his excitement although he tried very hard. He was anxious to get the evening on the way. Dee opened the door, and for a moment, the sight of her literally took his breath away. Her dark red, floor-length gown was cut lower than any dress he had seen her wear, exposing the beauty and smoothness of her skin. Her lips were full and ripe with a color that matched her dress. He couldn't fight the urge to kiss her.

"No, Tony," she said, turning her head. "You will destroy my make-up." Her hair was up, making her look more mature, and she wore the earrings Tony gave her as a birthday present.

"Dee, my God, you are so beautiful, wow! The entire family except Delores, was standing behind Dee watching Tony's reaction, and Mrs. Davis was very pleased and proud. Eli and Jan joked with Tony about his "monkey suit".

As they prepared to leave, Mrs. Davis said, "Wait a minute. There is something missing. Follow me, Dee," as they went into Dee's room. When they were out of sight, Eli rushed to the kitchen to get the roses Tony had brought earlier and gave them to Tony.

When Dee and Mrs. Davis returned to the living room, Tony held out the roses. Dee was overwhelmed.

"Oh, Tony," she sighed. "They are so beautiful." Looking at her mother, she asked, "Aren't they, Mother? Oh, Mother, you knew didn't you?" She reached for Tony's hands, holding them. "Oh, Tony, this is the greatest moment of my entire life."

Dee's eyes were getting cloudy as always in similar situations. She was excited, the family was excited, and Tony was excited; the evening was off to a fantastic start.

Jan joked, "Here come the tears and there goes the make-up."

"That's right," warned Mrs. Davis. "Girl, don't you start. You are going to ruin your face."

Eli, with a little humor, said, "Her face is already ruined." Everyone laughed, and Dee was able to hold back the flow of tears. Ted was close by observing and enjoying all of the fuss.

"You all have a good time. You two really do make a lovely pair," Mrs. Davis offered very profoundly.

Tony was a perfect gentleman with Dee. This was their first formal, and he could hardly bear to look away from her. He had never seen her so ravishingly beautiful. He made such a fuss over her that she became embarrassed. "Tony, I am the same girl you met midway through the seventh grade, with just a little more make-up, a new dress, and a different hairdo. Anyway, I am happy that you are pleased because I did it for you."

They bestowed each other with praises all evening. No doubt, the prom was a gala affair. Some of the girls Tony knew well were not easily recognized all dressed up. Many of the girls wanted to dance with Tony including several of his teachers. His reputation as a dancer was well known. Dee danced or talked with friends while Tony socialized.

In the past, she never seemed to mind him giving attention to others, but Tony had forgotten that this night was like no other.

"Tony, I have never complained about sharing you, but tonight is different. It is very special, and I want you all to myself."

"You are right, honey. I am sorry. I promise not to let you out of my reach anymore tonight," he agreed.

About eleven, Rhodes found Dee and Tony. "Let's go join Tom and Becky," he suggested.

They all found a place safe from the ears of others. "We need to leave in fifteen minutes. We have about a one-and-a-half-hour drive ahead of us. We will meet at Ray's Drive-In at one, sooner if you can, girls. We guys will be there no later than twelve thirty," urged Tom.

By twelve thirty everyone had met, paired off, and headed for the cabins with Tom and Becky leading the way.

"This night will be branded into my memory forever as the very best night of my life. Tony, the prom was great, being with you right now is great, this trip is great. Life is great," Dee shouted as if telling the world. She snuggled close to Tony as he put his arms around her shoulders, his hand touching her breast.

"Dee, you know, I have never felt so happy, either. So much has happened to us, yet, I really can't remember not loving you. I can't imagine us not being in love. I can't imagine life without your love. All of this is like a dream come true," he said, as he kissed the top of her head. The ride to the cabins was filled with gentle touches and tender words of love and desire.

As the cars stopped, Tom opened a gate apparently to the property where the cabins were located. Tony thought that time had passed awfully fast, but after checking his watch, the trip had taken an hour and twenty minutes. Tom motioned the cars inside, and he secured the gate. Although the moon was big and bright, it was difficult to get a scenic view of the property. As they parked at the cabins, Tony realized that he didn't remember any road or turn on the journey.

Tom and Becky took the smaller cabin with Rhodes and Susan sharing the larger cabin with Tony and Dee. The inside of the cabin looked better than most of the houses in Tony's neighborhood with all of the modern conveniences. The sleeping areas were on opposite sides of the cabin separated by a huge living, cooking, and game area with a fireplace. Everyone went to their respective sleeping areas agreeing to start off the day with a walk of the grounds.

Dee and Tony were too excited to sleep. "Gee, our first time spending an entire night together." Dee pondered, "When you see what I look like in the morning, or find out that I have bad breath, this may be our last," she teased.

"Don't give me that," Tony responded as they wrestled playfully on the bed. "You are not getting away from me no matter what," he assured her.

They played and talked for a while before deciding to go to bed. Dee flung herself onto the bed. "Tony, I want you to undress me and tuck me in bed."

He laughed, "Okay, but you will have to do me the honor tomorrow night."

Dee agreed, but she didn't tell him that she was going to make it difficult. She lay completely limp making Tony struggle to remove each garment. After a while, he decided to make it difficult for her. In between removing a piece of clothing, he would touch, kiss, and caress some of her most sensitive areas. After removing her blouse, he kissed and gently stroked her stomach and navel and proceeded to her ears, neck, and her breast through her bra. Before removing her skirt, he began rubbing her inner thighs with one hand while unsnapping her bra with the other.

She continued to remain limp under his extreme pressure although it was very difficult. It had been over twenty minutes since he removed her skirt and bra, leaving only her panties. He was passionately engulfed, kissing and caressing her from head to toe.

Eventually, she pulled his lips to hers and whispered, "You are not playing fair, Tony. You were supposed to undress me, not drive me crazy."

Their lips met in a deep, searing kiss. She pulled away to remove his sweater. "I'll bet you are surprised that I could control myself with the pressure you were putting on me. If you are not surprised, I am, and I will never be able to do it again. By the way, you are not finished, and I am not tucked in bed yet."

Tony finished undressing then returned to Dee lying on the bed. He lifted her, pulled the covers back, and laid her gently in bed. As he laid her in bed, she took his hand, threw back the covers, and drew him close. They began to touch and embrace until their passion and desires mounted to new heights. Dee began to tremble and shake all over.

"Tony," she sighed. "I want you now," she begged and rushed him into position. Their movement, their joy, and the sounds of love filled the morning as they found total fulfillment. Sleep, no longer evasive, came in abundance.

Awakened and startled by the pounding on the door, they sprang up in bed. "Say, you two lovebirds, get up. Tom and Becky will have breakfast ready in thirty minutes," Rhodes continued. "Are you two awake?"

"Yes," shouted Tony. "We'll be there shortly."

He and Dee jumped out of bed, showered together, made love, showered separately, and went to breakfast in forty-five minutes. As they opened the cabin door, they were in awe of the beauty they saw. The greenery, the birds, the wildlife, the water, and the air were astounding. They looked at each other and smiled not needing words to share what was in their hearts and minds. Taking each other's hands, they leisurely strolled to the other cabin.

Words were not needed to express the majestic beauty they had witnessed. Breakfast was fun. Everyone was still excited. Each couple would take turns cooking for the two days. Tom gave a tour of the grounds which were large and impressive, including a boat ride around the lake. The grounds had three picnic areas and a large recreation site with a covered canopy. Dee was breathless with excitement and wonderment. After the tour and a short rest, lounging on the pier, Dee and Rhodes decided to fish while everyone else relaxed on the pier listening to the water and watching the birds.

In the early evening, everyone gathered on the patio to listen to music and talk.

"Listen, you guys," Tom called out, "don't bother cooking for Becky and me. We may just get lost for the next day so help yourselves to everything. It is really great having good friends to share times like this. Thanks for coming."

"Stop, Tom, you are going to have Dee crying," teased Tony.

Dee was somewhat embarrassed. "Tony and my family tease me a lot because I am a sentimental slob," explained Dee.

"So am I, Tom is, too, but he hides it well," offered Becky.

"Since that leaves only four of us, I am all for each of us taking care of separate eating plans because Susan and I would just like to be by ourselves as much as possible," Rhodes suggested.

"After all, we came up here to get away, didn't we?"

Everyone going their separate ways was just what Dee and Tony wanted. "That's fine with Dee and me. What time are we leaving tomorrow?" asked Tony.

"Rhodes and I have to be at home by seven tomorrow evening, and don't forget, I have to take Becky and Dee home. It would be better for Rhodes and me if we could leave about two-thirty, no later than three," suggested Susan. Everyone agreed.

It had been a long day, and Dee looked tired. "Tony, if you don't mind, I am going to bed after I shower."

"Sweetheart," Tony responded with a playful attitude, "aren't you forgetting something? Last night was your night, and this is my night, remember?"

"You are right," admitted Dee, "but how would you like a better deal?"

Tony was rather suspicious of Dee's motives. "Okay, tell me about the deal you have in mind, but I will tell you now, it had better be real good."

Dee's games or deals were always exciting and interesting. Tony knew that he was sure to accept whatever deal or game she had in mind.

"Here is the deal," she said. "Instead of undressing you, I will shower every inch of your body. What do you think?"

Tony acted as if he was weighing his choices before declaring, "I'll take it! I'll take it!"

As the evening passed, they talked about the events of the day and how exciting and wonderful the trip had been.

Dee decided she wanted to undress Tony. "A deal is a deal," she said. After they both were undressed and in the shower, they embraced and held each other for almost ten minutes before she began to shower with him looking on. She handed him the towel and soap. "Here, make yourself useful, do my back."

He took the soap and towel. "I was being useful."

Dee disagreed, "You were gawking."

"Come on, Dee, let's just say that I was admiring and desiring your beautiful body."

"Okay, I take it back. You were being useful, but I still want you to do my back," she urged as they played and teased.

Tony didn't stop with her back. He was soaping her all over, and she loved every stroke. "Say, I am supposed to be doing the washing, and you were just supposed to do my back, remember?"

"You are right; it's your turn," he agreed.

As Dee began to soap him down, he knew immediately that he would not have the kind of control she had shown the night before as he found it impossible to keep his hands to himself.

"Now, Tony, you behave. I didn't interrupt you last night so you just relax. Down boy," she teased.

After the long and intimate shower, they lay in each others arms.

"Dee, you are simply great. How do you make me feel so strong? As I have told you many times before, I have never gotten enough of you. Do you realize that?" he asked.

"Honey, I can't explain what we do to each other," she sighed. "I just want to love you as long and as much as you will let me; I am hoping that will be forever. Oh, Tony, I love you more than I can begin to explain. You are my life."

They talked for hours, ending the night as they had the night before, consumed in rapturous bliss.

It was almost noon when Tony and Dee awakened. When he opened his eyes, she was looking at him with that warm, sensuous look he had seen many times.

"Tony, I don't want us to leave. I don't want to go back," she pleaded.

He put his arms around her holding her very tightly, trying to console her. "Dee, I know, honey, but you know we have to go home. I also hate to leave. It has been heaven, you've been heaven, and don't worry. There is no reason why our love can't continue as it is now. When we leave this place, we are not going to lose anything. This will be a beautiful memory as long as we live," he continued to hold her, kissing away her tears, but never letting go.

They remained in bed until it was time to leave. They were fulfilled, satisfied, content, happy, and very much in love. As they walked outside to leave, he noticed Dee standing, staring at the surroundings then turning to look at the cabin.

"Tony, let's do something like this again someday."

It seemed to take much longer to return to Ray's Drive-In than it did on the way to the lakes. Dee was very subdued for almost the entire trip except for the last few miles.

"Tony, this experience we've had this weekend has been more special than I can begin to say, and I know that you feel as I do, but there is something bothering me," her tone was very serious, even her expression.

"What's wrong, honey? You look upset. Sweetheart, I thought everything was fine. What's wrong, talk to me, please," he begged.

"Well, nothing is really wrong and everything is fine. It's just that we have done everything together. I've given myself to you every time you have wanted me. I haven't held anything back. My question is, with all we have experienced, what's left for the honeymoon? With you leaving, what happens if there is no honeymoon? Do you see what I am saying, Tony?"

"Yes, Dee, I see what you are saying. All I can say is that the only way we won't have a honeymoon is if you don't want a honeymoon. I will always love you, and I will definitely come back to you."

"Dee, your mother told us that it wouldn't be easy, and I believe her, but I am not worried as much as I hate leaving. I will come back to you," he emphasized.

Dee seemed pleased and satisfied as she always did with Tony's explanations. The girls got into the car with Susan. Dee promised to call as soon as she thought he was home. The guys talked a while before departing. Tony expressed his deep gratitude to Tom before they parted.

CHAPTER

XII

The last three days of school were a waste; nothing was accomplished. Time was passing at a rapid pace with just five days before Tony would be leaving for the army. He and Dee both were very depressed about his pending departure. They were overcome with panic, but they knew the day of departure was coming, and there was no place to run or hide from it. Thursday evening would be their last night together for some time to come. He had invited her over because he knew Marie and Clettis would be at church. He had said goodbye to other friends and relatives. Friday, before he took the train to Chicago, he would sell his car. To make matters worse, he was supposed to leave on Monday before it was moved up to Friday. Both he and Dee were very unhappy.

"Hey, Sis," Tony whispered, pulling Marie aside. "Please don't rush home from church tonight."

Marie looked at him and smiled. She had been everything to him, a friend, sister, and a mother. He loved her dearly. He knew that he would miss her. Mrs. Davis was very warm and friendly when he called for Dee. Tony said goodbye to Eli, Jan, and Ted in case they would be in bed when he took Dee home.

"Tony, we have had our differences, and sometimes things have been real tough, but I wish the best for you, and I will remember you in my prayers. Don't forget to write us sometimes. Take care of yourself," Mrs. Davis concluded.

Dee and Tony, knowing that it would be their last night for a long while, were dedicated to making it something special. Tony was surprised when Dee was not her passionate self.

"Tony, I am going to ask you for a big favor, and please try to understand. I know you want to make love and I do as well, but not right now. I don't know if we have as much as we think we have without sex. Let's not have sex tonight, Tony. Let's prove that we have the strength to love each other without sex." She was having difficulty trying to explain herself because she was trying to determine how well Tony was receiving her suggestion.

"Dee, do you realize how long we may be apart?" he was becoming a little annoyed.

"Yes, I do. If we have to do without it a year, one night isn't going to make a difference. Look, honey," she reasoned, coming close, putting her arms around his neck, "if you really don't understand, I will do whatever you want, but remember, Tony, I have never refused you anything. Now I need you to do something for me. Something that is very important to me. What are you going to do?" she asked, fearing that he would not understand.

Tony was becoming less disappointed the more he realized how important it was to Dee. He realized that she had never asked much of him. He smiled and put his arms around her waist.

"Can I kiss you?" he joked.

"Yes, yes, yes! Oh, Tony, you do understand! You are wonderful! Thank you Tony, I know this is difficult for you." She was all smiles as she sat in his lap. They talked about how they would handle the separation, and their plans for the future.

Tony found it impossible to sleep on his last night. He and Marie spent much of the night talking. Since she had been alone while Clettis was in Korea, she gave Tony some relevant suggestions. She encouraged him to write to Dee as much as possible. The next morning, he went to visit his mother before selling his car. He and Peter would be catching the same train to Chicago.

Marie and Dee went to the train station with Tony. Liz and Peter were saying their goodbyes. Tony said goodbye to Marie as he and Dee left for him to board the train.

"Don't say goodbye to me, Tony, because I know it's not goodbye. We will be together before you know it. Don't forget that there is a girl waiting and depending on you to return." Dee was talking unusually fast, trying to say everything before the train left.

Tony was hoping that she didn't start crying, but deep within, he knew that she would. "Dee, I will write at least six days a week, okay?" he promised, trying to lift her spirits.

"ALL ABOARD!"

When those words were echoed, their eyes became fixed on each other as Dee began to cry holding on to Tony.

In trying to reassure and console her, Tony was unable to hold back his tears. "Come on, Dee, don't cry." They were both filled with tears. "Everything will be fine, I promise."

Marie had come to help calm Dee. "Tony, do you really have to go? What can they do if you don't go? Why can't you go later? I really don't want you to go. When am I going to see you again? Oh Tony, please don't go," she was shaking and crying almost hysterically.

Tony held her one last time. They kissed. As he boarded the train, he saw Marie still trying to console Dee, holding her. He watched until they were out of sight and wondered, holding back the tears, when he would return and if things would ever be the same again.

THE END

CPSIA information can be obtained
at www.ICGtesting.com
Printed in the USA
LVHW032112260121
677513LV00002B/180